Desperate Choices

Desperate CHOICES

By
KATHY IVAN

COPYRIGHT

Desperate Choices – Original Copyright © September 2010 by Kathy Ivan

Cover by Elizabeth Mackay of EMGRAPHICS

Release date: February 2020
Print Edition

All Rights Reserved

DESPERATE CHOICES

When New Orleans police declare private investigator Max Lamoreaux's missing godson a runaway, he reaches out to former flame Theresa Crawford for help. Her specialized skills have proven key to unlocking past investigations. Time hasn't diminished their powerful chemistry, but Theresa's secrets drove them apart once before. As they work together, will shadows from her past destroy their last chance at happiness?

BOOKS BY KATHY IVAN

NEW ORLEANS CONNECTION SERIES

Desperate Choices

Connor's Gamble

Relentless Pursuit

Ultimate Betrayal

Keeping Secrets

Sex, Lies and Apple Pies

Deadly Justice

Wicked Obsession

Hidden Agenda

Spies Like Us

Fatal Intentions

New Orleans Connection Series Box Set: Books 1-3

New Orleans Connection Series Box Set: Books 4-7

CAJUN CONNECTION SERIES

Saving Sarah

Saving Savannah

Saving Stephanie

Guarding Gabi

LOVIN' LAS VEGAS SERIES

It Happened In Vegas

Crazy Vegas Love

Marriage, Vegas Style

A Virgin In Vegas

Vegas, Baby!

Yours For The Holidays
Match Made In Vegas
One Night In Vegas
Last Chance In Vegas
Lovin' Las Vegas (box set books 1-3)

OTHER BOOKS BY KATHY IVAN

Second Chances (Destiny's Desire Book #1)
Losing Cassie (Destiny's Desire Book #2)

Dear Reader,

Welcome to The Big Easy! Don't you just love New Orleans and all the people and places (especially the amazing food), and everything the city has to offer? I think another visit to this fair city is in my future!

Desperate Choices is the first book I wrote in my New Orleans Connection series, and I simply fell in love with the city and its people and unique places, and kept coming back, book after book, for the entire series.

In Desperate Choices, as with all of the New Orleans Connection Series and the Cajun Connection Series, you'll find a unique blend of suspense, romance, and intrigue set in the heart of New Orleans, filled with alpha heroes oozing Southern charm and the strong women they love.

So, sit back and hold on tight for a roller coaster ride of nail-biting intrigue and sensual tension with Desperate Choices.

As they say in New Orleans—*Laissez les bons temps rouler!*

Kathy Ivan

EDITORIAL REVIEWS

"Kathy Ivan's books are addictive, you can't read just one."

—Susan Stoker, NYT Bestselling Author

"Kathy Ivan's books give you everything you're looking for and so much more."

—Geri Foster, USA Today and NYT Bestselling Author of the Falcon Securities Series

"In Shiloh Springs, Kathy Ivan has crafted warm, engaging characters that will steal your heart and a mystery that will keep you reading to the very last page."

—Barb Han, *USA TODAY* and Publisher's Weekly Bestselling Author

"This is the first I have read from Kathy Ivan and it won't be the last."

—Night Owl Reviews

"I highly recommend Desperate Choices. Readers can't go wrong here!"

—Melissa, Joyfully Reviewed

"I loved how the author wove a very intricate storyline with plenty of intriguing details that led to the final reveal…"

—Night Owl Reviews

Desperate Choices—Winner 2012 International Digital Award—Suspense

Desperate Choices—Best of Romance 2011 –Joyfully Reviewed

DEDICATIONS AND ACKNOWLEDGEMENTS

To Jane Graves for reigniting my love of writing and helping me realize I could do it. To my sister, Mary Sullivan, for her unwavering belief that I could write a good story and would one day be published. Looks like you were right, Sis. Lastly, this book is dedicated to my mother, Betty Sullivan. She instilled in me the joy of reading at an early age and a love of romance, no matter the genre. Although I lost her before she could see me become a published writer, I know she's smiling, thrilled to see me take this leap into a world she loved so much. Miss you bunches, Mom.

More about Kathy and her books can be found at

WEBSITE:
www.kathyivan.com

Follow Kathy on Facebook at
www.facebook.com/kathyivanauthor

Follow Kathy on Twitter at
twitter.com/@kathyivan

Follow Kathy at BookBub
bookbub.com/profile/kathy-ivan

NEWSLETTER SIGN UP

Don't want to miss out on any new books, contests, and free stuff? Sign up to get my newsletter. I promise not to spam you, and only send out notifications/e-mails whenever there's a new release or contest/giveaway. Follow the link and join today!

http://eepurl.com/baqdRX

Desperate
CHOICES

By
KATHY IVAN

Chapter One

She should have locked the door.

Theresa Crawford watched the man close the door behind him with a firm but solid click. Big trouble—she could sense it. Darkness radiated from him in waves.

"Hello, Max." Her soft-spoken greeting broke the silence. She remained seated behind the table draped with various multicolored scarves, studying the man in front of her. Though she'd known him for over ten years, he was too complex to say she knew him well.

Without waiting for an invitation, Max Lamoreaux walked the few steps it took to reach her. Pulling out the chair opposite he sat, straddling it. His long lean frame filled the delicate white chair. His gaze locked with hers.

A familiar sense of anticipation flittered through her like butterfly wings. The hairs on the back of her neck stood at attention. Theresa felt like a frightened animal right before the fight or flight response kicks in. She wasn't sure which she'd do. Given their history, probably fight.

As Max started to speak she held up her hand and indicated for him to wait. Rising from her chair she walked over to a browsing couple, the only customers in the store, and politely informed them the shop was closing early.

At the door, with deliberate measured movements, she turned the lock and flipped the sign hanging in the glass-paneled door to Closed.

Glancing back, she paused and inhaled a long steadying breath before exhaling slowly. Her palms slid down the front of her flowing skirt, wiping away the traces of nervous moisture. Max coming to her shop? Definitely not good.

Facing the table, she opened her psychic channels. Maybe she could get a glimpse of why he was here. Nothing. Max had amazing natural shields. Right now they were firmly in place, solid as steel and just as impenetrable.

Theresa sat and looked up to meet Max's intent stare. She nodded, allowing him to proceed.

The tight press of his lips along with the deep crevice between his strong brows conveyed his discomfort and anger. An uncommon combination for him, she thought. He still hadn't spoken, staring at her with those steely ice-gray eyes. That look sent rippling, sizzling sensations through her. Underneath it all, despite their past, there lurked a hunger which refused to be hidden.

Theresa broke eye contact with difficulty. She could get lost in the storm clouds of his stare. In fact she had, on more occasions than she cared to remember. Glancing down, she spotted the thick manila envelope he'd laid on the table.

Well, that explains it. He's on a case.

"What do you want, Max?" Theresa noted her hesitancy and took a cleansing breath, focused on curbing the underlying nervousness in her tone.

"Same old Theresa, right to the point. As always."

"Look, no small talk, Max. It never works for us. Just get to the point. What do you want?"

With a gentle shove, Max pushed the envelope across the table. She stared at him, waiting. This was his show. He was the one with the questions.

"Okay, we both know I'm not comfortable being here. I wouldn't have come, but Remy insisted. You know how persuasive he can be when he thinks he's right."

Theresa's brow quirked. Remy was Max's brother and had been her best friend for more than ten years. Remy knew how much she hated using her gift, especially around Max. His skepticism had caused hurtful, angry words between them several times.

"You know I don't believe in all this psychic mumbo-jumbo crap. But I'm at a complete dead end. I'm willing to try *anything* to get a new lead, a direction to take this case."

Theresa noted the almost undetectable tremor in his voice, a true indicator of the frustration he must be feeling. She rubbed the bridge of her nose with her fingertips before speaking. "I'm well aware of your feelings about psychics, Max, so don't embellish. Give me the facts."

Max's presence overpowered the compact space. He exuded a powerful masculine aura, making everything around him seem insignificant. He'd always done that whenever he entered a room. She felt an instinctive pull toward him, as powerful today as the day she'd met him. Some things never changed. Looking at him stirred up feelings and memories hard to push aside. He'd always been able to twist her inside-out with a hint of his smile. *Just stop it. Now's not the time.*

"A week ago I got a call from an old college buddy, David Saunders, in a panic because his son was missing. He never came home after work."

Oh, no. Her entire body tensed at the mention of a missing child, her fingers clenching into fists as every muscle in her body contracted in an instinctive effort at self-preservation. *Not again. I can't work on another missing child case.*

"How old is he?" she asked quietly, striving to speak over her rising panic.

"Tommy turned seventeen a couple of weeks ago." There was a hint of warmth in Max's tone, his affection for the boy evident. "Of course, David called the police immediately. The NOPD started an investigation, and I've been monitoring the situation. Yesterday, the police classified the case as a runaway."

He folded his arms and leaned forward, resting both forearms along the backrest of the chair. "There hasn't been a ransom demand. His motorcycle hasn't been seen."

Springing up from the chair, Max paced, a habit he'd had for as long as she'd known him. Theresa watched his backward and forward momentum. She knew he did some of his best thinking when he walked. He moved like a coiled panther, all lean muscle and leashed power. She followed his movements, all the while listening as he recited facts.

This felt off somehow. Max wasn't verbose at the best of times, yet now he seemed almost…talkative.

"He's a good kid who's had a rough time. David moved

out a few months ago, and Tommy's been having some problems at school. Grades dropping, skipping a few classes. David said he and his wife fought with Tommy the morning he went missing. Tommy blew up at them before he left. Then he never came home. No calls. Nothing."

Max stopped in front of her. His eyes locked with hers. Theresa looked away, closing her eyes to block out the pain she read on his face.

"David swears Tommy wouldn't run away. I believe him. For God's sake, he's my godson. He's a responsible, well-adjusted teenager. The cops said they'll leave it an open case for now, but they're without leads, too."

Eyes closed, Theresa listened quietly, taking in the information. More, though, she heard the emotions his voice carried. His conviction Tommy hadn't run away. One thing was clear: Max was scared.

"The parents contacted the National Hotline for Missing Children?" Theresa opened her eyes, meeting his. "What about his friends? Could somebody be helping him hide out—trying to frighten his parents?" At the skeptical look on Max's face, she changed tactics.

"Right, not hiding out. So, you're sure somebody's got him? What exactly do you think I can tell you?"

Max pointed to the envelope in front of Theresa. "We know what time he left his job and the route he takes home every night. The police scoured every inch of road, from the video store to his house. There was a cell phone on the ground a few miles outside New Orleans. It was his. Right now it's the only clue we've got."

He paused and ran a hand through his tousled black hair. "I didn't want to get Remy involved since he works for the NOPD, so I had a buddy at the police department get me the phone from the evidence locker. Totally unethical and against every rule, but he owed me. I've got it for the next 24 hours, then it has to go back."

Max picked up the envelope and upended its contents. A black-and-chrome phone tumbled onto the table, clattering to rest on the colorful scarves.

Theresa didn't reach for it. She backed away, her spine pressed against her chair. She stared at the object sitting innocuously on the scarf-covered tabletop, her body frozen.

Max squatted beside her, resting his hand on her knee. Frustration and pain filled his voice. She couldn't drag her eyes from his face. His eyes swirled with emotion. Pain. Grief. Worry.

"Okay, Ms. Psychic. Remy's so damn sure you can help. Work your magic. Perform your voodoo or whatever the hell you do. Where is Tommy and how on God's earth do we get him back?"

★　★　★

Behind the wheel of the car, Max angled his head and watched Theresa. She sat silent and unmoving, just as she had since they'd left her shop. His gaze slid slowly along the length of her, and he definitely liked what he saw. He never paid much attention to her when she and Remy first began hanging out together. She'd been way too young. He'd rarely been home then, staying in Shreveport while attending LSU.

Max didn't really understand Theresa and Remy's friendship. They were so diametrically different, yet their friendship endured all these years.

Theresa had spent a lot of time at their house, all the holidays, birthdays, even family reunions. She was practically a member of the family, at least to everybody but him. He'd never had the remotest familial thought about her. When he looked at her, she set him aflame.

Every damn time there was a family get-together, she'd been included. Until about a year ago. Things started to change then. He stopped seeing her as Remy's best friend. Instead he saw a sexy, vibrant, eye-catching woman. A woman he wanted in a primitive, gut-wrenching and wholly masculine way. His body ached with wanting her. He'd been avoiding her like the plague ever since. A relationship was a complication he couldn't afford in his life right now.

"Pull over here." Her voice drew his attention back to the road. He angled the car over to the side of the pavement. Coasting to a stop, he swiveled to face the passenger side, watching Theresa closely.

"Why here?" he asked in a deceptively quiet voice, careful to betray nothing. An amazing coincidence. She'd told him to stop at the exact location the police discovered Tommy's cell phone. *Just a lucky guess. Doesn't mean a damn thing.*

Opening the passenger door, Theresa stepped from the car. Max got out and walked around the front to join her where she stood. He watched her take several steps forward and then backtrack. Her eyelids were shuttered, as if by closing them, she could obscure her surroundings.

For a few tense moments, he watched and waited. In a whispered tone, she finally spoke. "Give me the cell phone."

Quiet resolve and determination filled her face. Reaching through the passenger-side window, he plucked the manila envelope from the front seat and handed it to her. Then he stood back and watched.

Theresa slowly opened the clasp on the envelope, her movements tentative, a slight trembling in her fingers. She didn't want to be involved in this case. She had a bad feeling about this, a really bad feeling. Mentally bracing herself as she reached inside, she grasped the cell phone. She lifted it and held it in her right hand, her fingers sliding around the metal and plastic. It felt cool to her touch. Switching her grip to both hands now, the envelope drifted unnoticed to the grass.

Images began to form. Slowly at first, they gained substance as she allowed the psychic energy to wash over her. It happened like that sometimes. Some visions came in a great flash, immediate and precise in detail, crystal clear and sharp. Other things were vague, fuzzy, out of focus.

The closest she'd ever come to describing it was a near-sighted person without their glasses, nearly blind. With tremendous concentration, she could sometimes get images to slowly and steadily come into focus.

Even though it was late afternoon, in her mind's eye it was nearing twilight. That dusky time between day and night where everything fades to shades of gray, black and white.

She extended her extrasensory flow, hearing nothing except the sounds of nature. Crickets chirped, mosquitoes buzzed, an occasional bird lifted in flight with a swoosh of its wings. The normal sounds of a Louisiana evening.

Things began coalescing into definition. She stood alongside a motorbike. The motor wasn't running.

She allowed her psychic senses run free. In the distance, she heard an engine. Its growl grew louder as it approached. A vehicle pulled to the side of the road a short distance ahead of where she stood beside the bike.

"Theresa," Max interrupted. Never opening her eyes, she raised her finger to her mouth, motioning for quiet.

She concentrated on the vehicle, but as hard as she tried, it wouldn't come into a clear image. She could only determine it was a light color and large. *Focus,* she whispered in her mind. *Go deeper. Bring it into focus.*

A sudden jolt broke her concentration. Her neck snapped back, jarring her from the vision and back into reality. Theresa stared up at Max's face inches from hers, so close she could feel the warmth of his breath against her skin. His grasp on her shoulders felt firm yet insistent.

"Theresa." A hint of anxiety filled Max's normally placid voice. "Theresa. Snap out of it."

"What's wrong, Max?"

"What's wrong? You were standing there, barely breathing, shaking like a leaf, and you ask me 'What's wrong?'" Max's hold on her eased and she watched him run a hand across his eyes. "What the hell just happened?"

The vision vanished, faded away like mist evaporating.

Nothing left but the daylight surrounding her and Max. She handed him the phone and managed to stagger a couple of steps, resting her hip against the hood of the car.

Her body trembled, exhaustion enveloping her like a heavy cloak. This was one of the reasons she hated this kind of reading. It wiped her out, leaving her emotionally and physically drained.

"There's not a lot I can tell you, Max. I saw the bike at the side of the road. Right there." She pointed. "It wasn't running. I couldn't tell why not. I didn't get the impression there was anything mechanically wrong, but…"

She took a few steps away from the car and glanced toward the woods. They were dense, thick and mysterious, yet no sense of danger emanated from them. Filtered sunlight poured through the few leaves, wiping away all trace of the twilight hues from her vision.

"Another vehicle pulled over there." She gestured toward the road again, indicating an area about twenty feet beyond where his car was parked. "It was large, light in color. Maybe white or a light yellow or tan, I couldn't tell. It stopped. I sensed a brief moment of fear, but just as quickly it was gone. Tommy felt relief. He didn't seem afraid. He seemed thankful, maybe even happy."

Theresa looked up into Max's eyes for the first time since the vision ended and met his gray-eyed gaze.

"Max, whoever took Tommy wasn't a stranger. It was somebody he knew."

Chapter Two

Tommy jerked awake, sucking huge gasps of air into his struggling lungs. His heart raced, the rapid beat pounded in his ears. Sweat covered his body.

Same stupid dream again.

He rose from his rumpled bed, his breathing finally slowing, and stretched his arms above his head. Reaching down, his hand scratched lightly at his bare stomach and he stifled a yawn. Taking that first step away from the bed, he paced the floor of his prison. Back and forth, he dragged the chain behind him as he walked. He walked as far as he was able, changed direction and returned back to where he'd started. Silver links tethered him within the room, making escape impossible.

He knew—because he'd tried everything.

When he'd first opened his eyes, his initial reaction was disbelief. Gray cinderblock walls hemmed in the cramped, boxy room. He'd been lying on the floor. He'd jumped up and banged on the door only to feel the heavy slap of the chain against his skin.

"Let me out," he'd screamed at the top of his lungs. "You can't keep me here."

Nobody answered.

He was chained up like an animal. He had no idea where or why, but he sure as hell knew by whom.

He'd never told a soul, but his biggest nightmare had always been the fear of being trapped alone. Now it was his living reality.

He looked around the room, once again noting the lack of any windows. There were two doors in what he referred to as his "cage." One led to the bathroom, the other led to freedom. One he had access to, the other was denied.

The room was obviously a converted garage with cement floors and cinderblock walls. In actuality it probably wasn't a bad living space, might even be considered a studio apartment. There was a kitchenette complete with a refrigerator and sink. A single cabinet held a stash of snacks.

A miniscule bathroom occupied one corner. On the other side of the main room a mishmash of furnishings, an overstuffed chair, a rickety end table and a state-of-the-art television. There was even a DVD player with an assortment of DVDs.

Against the far wall stood a single brass bed. The headboard and footboard were heavily bolted to the floor. The manacle encircling his right ankle was fastened to one leg of the footboard.

He'd checked out every square inch of his confined space. There was nothing he could use as a weapon or to free himself. His kidnapper provided meals twice a day, brought in on a wicker tray with paper plates and flimsy plastic utensils.

Tommy mulled as he paced. He remembered his Suzuki

having a flat tire on the way home. After a really crappy day, he'd been pissed off because something so stupid would get him into even more trouble with his parents.

He remembered being scared spitless when the van pulled to a stop. Thoughts raced through his mind as he imagined the worst possible things that could happen. Child pornography. White slavery. Torture. Rape. Even death. Still, he'd put on a brave face. *Never let 'em see you sweat.* When he saw who got out of the van, his relief was almost palpable. *Thank God.*

They had chatted on the drive back toward New Orleans, heat blasting from the van's blowers. He felt comforted something had gone right for the first time that day. When they passed the first gas station with a mechanic still on duty, he looked at Steven. Before he could ask, Steven said he had one stop to make first. He knew a good mechanic who could fix the tire and wouldn't charge him. They needed to go to his house to get his friend's phone number. He asked if Tommy minded stopping for a minute. Free repairs? Who'd turn that down?

When they got to the house, Steven invited him in for something to drink. The next thing he remembered, he'd awoken in this room, chained up like a vicious junkyard dog.

Stupid, stupid, stupid. I have to be the biggest idiot in the world.

Everybody in and around New Orleans knew Steven Black. He was a general handyman and contractor. He even did the weekly maintenance on his parents' lawn. He'd never thought Steven would be capable of something this heinous.

Once more, Tommy pulled on the footboard, attempting to loosen the chain, the same futile effort he made hundreds of times daily. Even after almost a week, there was no give.

A sudden noise alerted Tommy he was no longer alone. His body tensed. He knew who it was. The key clicked in the lock. The door opened slowly.

Tommy watched in silence as Steven stepped across the threshold, a heavy burden in his arms wrapped securely within a blanket. Steven walked toward the brass bed and gently laid his bundle down. With infinite care, he unfurled the blanket. A head and shoulders appeared, followed by a faint groan.

Tommy's world seemed to freeze in stunned disbelief, his breath stuttering in his chest. Time seemed to slow to a crawl. *Dear God above,* he thought, his stare riveted to the now-occupied bed. *He's kidnapped somebody else.*

Chapter Three

Theresa glanced across the dinner table at Remy. He'd called earlier to find out how things had gone with his brother. More than that, though, she knew he was checking on her. Remy knew how emotionally and physically drained she became after a reading. Exhausted, she could barely function when she finished. Even now, several hours afterward, a bone-weary tiredness had set in. Still, for her best friend, she gave the illusion of coping.

Remy's faith and unshakable trust in her abilities almost convinced her she could help Max's case. He'd witnessed her gift many times over the years. He didn't have the same unsubstantiated disbelief Max did.

"Hey, sweetie. Spill it. What did you 'see'?" Remy smiled, his play on words filled with wry humor. He teased her openly about her gift. Most people were too uncomfortable around her, especially when they wanted her help.

"Not nearly enough." Theresa looked at Remy, marveling at their friendship. For more than ten years they had remained close. The bond between them surpassed any lack of a DNA connection. They were a living example of enduring friendship, triumphant over all odds.

She smiled at the waiter as he placed her meal in front of

her. Raising her water glass, she took a sip. She inhaled the fragrance of the seafood platter, glad Remy insisted she come to dinner.

Her eyes met Remy's and she gave him a wink.

"Max and I went to the spot where Tommy supposedly disappeared. I don't think I was much help, though. I sensed it was the last place he'd been. There wasn't any malevolence or evil there, Remy. Whatever happened didn't feel planned."

Theresa knew she could talk freely with Remy about the case. Besides being Max's brother and her best friend, he was also a detective with the New Orleans Police Department, working Vice.

The candlelight flickered softly, accentuating Remy's rugged appeal. His dark hair, nearly black, was brushed back from a sculptured, masculine face. Extremely long black lashes outlined his piercing amber eyes. Though they should have been feminine in appearance, on him they were anything but girlish. His nose was a touch sharp but lent character to his face.

His physical beauty was not what attracted her to him. His sharply cut physique wasn't the answer, either. His appeal had always been what was inside. His kindness. His spirit. His joy in life. But mostly his unconditional love for her.

Theresa shook her head, scattering thoughts about Remy's physical appearance, and refocused on the subject at hand. As attractive as Remy was, she had never been interested in him except as a friend. For her, it was always

Max.

She drew up when she realized she was comparing Remy to Max. *Stop thinking about Max. It's never going to happen.*

Remy snapped his fingers in front of her face. "Earth to Theresa. Anybody home?"

Startled, she blinked, realizing her thoughts had taken her far away from the present. The corners of her mouth quirked upwards. "Sorry, Remy. Lost in my thoughts again."

A familiar tingle flittered along Theresa's spine and probed at her psychic shields. Somebody watched her. She could feel his eyes. Her gaze traveled to the entrance of the restaurant. She cursed under her breath as she met Max's intent stare. His purposeful strides ate up the distance to their table.

Max reached out and clamped his hand on Remy's shoulder. "I called the house and *Maman* said I'd probably find you here. She said you were taking Theresa out for dinner."

Though he spoke to Remy, he stared intently at Theresa. His eyes perused her appearance in minute detail. Theresa's spine stiffened as she braced for Max's next words.

"What's up, bro?" Remy looked up at Max, concern written on his face.

"Actually I was looking for Theresa. I wanted to run something by her before I approached Tommy's parents."

"What?" Theresa asked.

"I want to take you to Tommy's house in the morning. Maybe being around so many of his personal things…it might give you additional material to work with. You know, get some 'vibes' from some of his stuff. Talk with his parents."

Max hesitated. "I haven't told his parents I've consulted a psychic. I wanted to check with you before I said anything."

"Why? Are you ashamed of me?" Theresa couldn't quite keep the piqued tone out of her voice. "I don't go around advertising the fact I'm psychic, but I don't hide it either. It's fine to tell them."

Max rocked back on his heels, one hand shoved into his pants pocket. "Fine. I'll pick you up about eight."

"Fine."

An awkward silence enveloped their table. Moments ticked by.

Theresa decided she needed to leave. She had spent enough time around Max today fighting his skepticism—and her overwhelming attraction to him. Their time apart hadn't dimmed her body's response to his. Distance was her answer.

She retrieved her purse from underneath her chair. "Remy, I'm going to call it a night, if you don't mind. I've got a bit of a headache, and I'm really not very hungry. I'll call you tomorrow, okay?"

Remy stood and pulled out her chair while motioning for the waiter to bring the check.

"No, Remy. Please stay and have dessert. Talk with Max. I'm going to walk home. It's just a couple of blocks, and the fresh air will clear my head."

Leaning in, she brushed a kiss against Remy's cheek, and then looked at Max. His icy stare met hers. There was something there, something she couldn't read. His shields slammed into place, tighter than ever.

"Goodnight, Max. I'll see you in the morning." Her skirt rustled, the hem swirling around her legs as she walked toward the door and out into the night.

★　★　★

"Well, crap. Talk about ruining a perfectly good dinner. Couldn't you have called her at home and left a message?" Remy slouched back in his chair, his fork pushing around the food on his barely touched plate. "You might as well join me. Misery loves company."

Remy again motioned for the waiter, who hurried over with his check. "Never mind, my brother's going to join me. What'll you have, Maxey?" Max winced at his brother's use of a name he hadn't answered to in years. He'd always hated his childhood nickname.

Max ordered a steak, baked potato and a cold beer before lounging back in the chair Theresa had vacated.

"Damn it, Remy, I didn't mean to run her off. I guess I wasn't thinking, period. This case has me going round in circles, chasing my tail. I can't catch a break. I'm so worried about Tommy, it's eating me up. There are so many rotten bastards out there. Anybody could have snatched him."

"I was asking Theresa how things went today when you interrupted. Was she any help?"

"Yes and no. I didn't give her much info. We drove to the exact spot where the police found his phone. It was like she watched it happen. She stood so still, barely moving."

Max knew he could tell his brother everything. That

wasn't what was bothering him. It was his own reaction when Theresa nearly stopped breathing. The sheer panic he'd felt, like a vise grip on his lungs squeezing tighter and tighter. He ran his hand across his chest now, remembering the sensation.

"I canvassed the scene while she talked, listening but not wholly concentrated on her. She paused for a minute. I didn't think anything of it. Until I looked at her." Reaching for the cold beer the waiter just delivered, he took a deep swallow. "Damn, Remy. It was like she stopped breathing. Not much scares me these days, but I'm telling you watching her like that, it scared the hell out of me."

Remy nodded at Max's words, his look compassionate. "Man, I'm sorry. It's rare for it to happen like that. I saw it once before, and it frightened the crap out of me, too."

"Is it normal?" Max asked. "You know her better than I do. Should I be worried about her working this case?"

"You'd have to ask her. I haven't let Theresa work on any more of my cases. Once was more than enough."

"Whoa, hold it. *You* told me to go to her. You're the one who convinced me she'd be able to help find Tommy."

"And I'm still convinced she can. Just because I won't allow her to work on my cases, doesn't mean she wouldn't be of benefit to you. Remember, I'm in Vice now, but back then, I worked Homicide. Way, way too traumatic for her."

Max grimaced, frowning slightly when Remy mentioned the Homicide Department. He'd worked Shreveport Homicide for several years before leaving under less than auspicious circumstances. It was still a raw area for him.

"I've seen what Theresa can do, Max. She's not always comfortable with her abilities, but when the situation warrants it, she does what's necessary to help others. She's a strong woman, but sometimes it overwhelms her."

"I'm worried enough about finding Tommy right now. I can't afford to worry about her, too. Another episode like today, and that's it." Max pushed his half-finished plate away and stood.

"Keep an eye on her, Remy." He hesitated as if he wanted to say more, then shook his head.

"G'night, bro."

Chapter Four

Early the next morning, Max pulled his car into the drive of the Saunders's house and cut the engine. He swiveled around in the seat to face Theresa, his thoughts conflicted. He was still worried about her working on this case. Maybe it was more than she could handle. She looked so pale. Shadows darkened the naturally pale skin beneath her eyes. The normal healthy luster of her flawless skin was absent, a telltale indicator of a sleepless night.

Clearly reading his expression, she offered, "Don't say it, Max. I'm fine." Theresa reached down and unbuckled her seatbelt, flicked the door handle and pushed it open. "Let's go."

Max joined her on the short walk up the pristine drive. The smell of freshly cut grass assailed his senses.

He noted the white pickup truck parked alongside the narrow drive, a local landscaper's logo painted on its side. The mechanized sounds of a lawnmower rumbled nearby. Max spotted Steven Black, a well-known local handyman, as he propelled the mower across the neatly manicured grass. Taking in the perfectly sculptured hedges and the neatly trimmed grass, Max guessed he was meticulous about his work. With a nod and a smile, Steven acknowledged their presence and kept on with his mowing.

Theresa waited on the front step and Max hurried to join her, rapping on the glass-paneled door. Mere moments passed before Suzanne Saunders opened it. Though he had seen her a few days prior, Max stared. She seemed to have aged ten years in that short time. Signs of sleeplessness and weight loss were apparent on her diminutive frame.

"Come on in." Always a gracious hostess, Suzanne stepped back and motioned for them to enter. David stood a few feet inside the foyer, deep shadows and lines furrowed his brow.

Suzanne extended her hand to Theresa, who shook it briefly. Looking at Max, she said, "I called David last night, after your call, and asked him to be here. This is Miss Crawford, I assume?" Max nodded.

"Max told me on the phone last night you claim you're some kind of a psychic, Ms. Crawford? I have to tell you I don't believe in those kinds of things. I'm more a believe-what-you-can-see-and-feel type person." Suzanne walked over and took David's hand in a bone-squeezing grip.

"At this point, regardless of what I think or believe," she said, "I'll try anything to find my son. Anything. Let us know what you need, and you've got it. We'll pay you whatever…" Her voice trailed off as she choked back tears.

Theresa smiled softly, her words gentle and calm. "Mrs. Saunders, I don't want your money. The only reason I'm here is Max thinks I might be of some help. I don't know if I will, but I'm going to try."

"David, how about we take Theresa up to Tommy's

room and let her look around, get a feel for things," Max interrupted. His hand rested just above the small of Theresa's back. His fingertips tingled at the slight contact, even though no bare skin touched. He drew in a shallow breath and inhaled the scent of honeysuckle, light and floral, combined with the underlying scent that was uniquely Theresa.

"Right this way, Ms. Crawford." David Saunders led Theresa and Max into the depths of the house and down a long hallway before stopping at the second doorway on the left.

"This is Tommy's room. We haven't touched anything in here since he went missing. Except for the bed. I keep finding Suzanne curled up on it, crying." His voice broke as he battled tears of his own. Max placed a comforting hand on David's shoulder, giving it a gentle squeeze.

"Don't worry. We're gonna find him. I promise you, we'll find him."

★　★　★

Opening the door, David took a step back, giving Theresa access to Tommy's room.

She walked forward slowly, absorbing her surroundings, taking in the details of Tommy Saunders's life. The bedroom was a typical teenage boy's room with pale blue walls accented by white trim, a full-sized bed, dresser, and shelves on the walls. A set of weights took up one-quarter of the far corner. Haphazardly scattered across the navy carpet, they were a testament to his rush through life. Teenagers, especially boys, weren't known for picking up after themselves, she thought.

Walking over to the shelves above the cherry dresser, she lightly ran her fingers across the items atop its polished surface. There were a few blue and red ribbons, a couple of trophies and a number of worn paperback books stacked on top. Science fiction classics, a couple of them her personal favorites. Smiling, she reached up and touched the back of one. She felt a faint tingle, but nothing specific.

She moved farther into the room and continued her perusal. Her eyes landed on a crumpled paper lying on the floor next to the headboard. Reaching down, she picked it up and smoothed out the wrinkles, noting the masculine handwriting.

"Looks like he did well in history." She handed the page to his father, watched him smile wistfully at the ninety-five percent score in red at the top of the page.

"Yeah, he loved history. It's one of the few classes he aced, even when the rest of his grades dropped." David's voice broke. He held the paper to his chest, his eyes filled with unshed tears. The sight of this grown man in so much pain touched Theresa. She wanted—no, she *needed* to help bring him some kind of peace.

"I want him home. I can't stand this. Not knowing where he is, if he's safe." David turned and left, the history paper still nestled over his heart.

Max walked over and perched on the foot of the bed, his hands braced behind him. "You getting anything?"

Theresa ignored him and took a few more steps around the room, stopping in front of the bedroom closet. She opened the door and cautiously ran her hand above the hanging garments, not quite touching them. Her hand stopped for a moment, her fingers still. She reached in and touched a sweater gently, then pulled back from it and continued to the next.

Closing the closet door, she turned back to Max. "I'm not getting anything new here, Max. Some of the things you already told me—anger at his parents' breakup, problems with school—but nothing else. Whatever happened to him, it's not connected to this house."

Max took a deep breath, exhaling slowly, and ran his fingers through his hair. "I didn't think you'd get anything, but I figured it was worth a shot. Damn." He stood and headed for the door.

Theresa followed, but stayed a short distance back so she wouldn't interfere while he talked with Tommy's parents. On hearing there was nothing new, Tommy's mother began crying silently. David moved around to her chair, and pulled her close to his side.

Bidding them a quiet but heartfelt goodbye, Max led Theresa out the front door and back toward his car. Steven had finished up with the yard work and was loading his equipment into the back of the pickup. Max turned toward Theresa.

"I need to speak with Steven for a minute." He reached into his pocket and pulled out his keys. "Why don't you go ahead and crank up the heater." Though it was only mid-

November, there was a definite chill in the early morning air. He watched her walk toward the car, before turning his attention to Steven.

"Morning, Black. Can I talk to you for a minute?" he asked.

Closing the tailgate of the pickup, Steven swung around to face him. "Sure. What can I do for you?"

"My name's Max Lamoreaux. I'm a friend of the Saunders's. Working for the family, I'm sure you've heard Tommy's missing?" At Steven's nod, Max continued.

"They've hired me to find him. Since you're around New Orleans so much with your work, I thought you might have heard something. Maybe one of his friends talking?"

"Sorry, Mr. Lamoreaux. I'm real sorry for what the Saunders are going through right now. They're a good family and don't deserve this. They've always been real good to me, hiring me year-round to keep after things, doing odd jobs for them."

Scratching the side of his balding head, he looked Max in the eye. "I can't rightly say I've heard anything. Couple of kids saying they thought he'd run away, 'cause that's what everybody else was saying. I don't believe it, though. Tommy's a good kid. He wouldn't hurt them like this."

Reaching into his wallet, Max pulled out a business card and handed it to Steven. "If you hear anything, no matter how trivial or unimportant you think it is, call me right away, okay? We need to find Tommy and bring him home safe."

He shook Steven's hand then walked back to his car and

got in. Toasty warmth poured from the vents and spread throughout the interior. He watched Theresa, noting her gaze on Steven as he got into his truck and pulled out of the driveway.

"Who's that man, Max?"

"Steven Black. He's a local handyman and landscaper. Why?"

"I don't know." Theresa leaned back in her seat and closed her eyes. "He just looked familiar. I guess I've seen him around town."

Chapter Five

Tommy sat on the floor, his back against the wall. He wrapped his arms around his bent knees as he stared at the unmoving form on the bed. She slept so peacefully. He couldn't tell if she was drugged or not. She hadn't stirred since she'd been placed there, as still and pale as a marble statue.

He was amazed Steven had brought somebody else here. Was she another captive, like him? Steven warned Tommy against bothering her. Told him not to touch her or even talk to her. At this point, Tommy knew to take Steven's not-so-veiled threats seriously. After all, look where he was.

A flicker of movement caught his eye and his gaze flew back to the bed. A low partially muffled moan followed. Tommy wasn't sure what to do, but figured any kind of action at this point was better than doing nothing.

He was so freakin' tired of being alone. Tired of spending days on end with nobody to talk to except Steven, who rarely spoke, just delivered his meals and checked to ensure his manacle was still intact and firmly fastened to the floor.

He stood and stretched, muscles stiff from inactivity. He'd sat on that hard cement floor far too long. He walked slowly to the foot of the single brass bed. The girl lay still now, but she was definitely waking up.

Tommy took a good long look at her. It had taken a while, but he recognized her. She looked familiar, in an I-know-I've-seen-you-before way. They went to the same high school—she was a year behind him.

He remembered seeing her in the school play the year before. She'd been one of the leads. At the time he thought she was pretty good and kinda cute.

He looked at her now. Her brown hair flowed across the pillow, highlights of golden blond surrounded her face. *Sunkissed.* That was the word people used about hair like hers. He remembered reading it in one of those magazines his mom left around the house.

Tommy slapped his open palm against his forehead. What a blockhead! He must be more brain-fried than he realized to be thinking about the colors in a girl's hair.

He inhaled sharply as her eyes flashed open, startling him. *They're green.* He smiled at her in friendly invitation.

"Who are you?" Her voice was low and breathy, the sound slightly scratchy from sleep. Tommy's gaze shifted from her eyes to her mouth. "What are you doing here?"

"I'm Tommy." He ran a nervous hand through his mussed hair and cleared his throat before repeating, "Tommy Saunders."

"Okay, Tommy Saunders. What are you doing in my room?"

"Your room?" Tommy was surprised at her revelation. Here all this time he'd thought it was his prison. "You live here?"

The girl stared at him, still lying back against the pillows. "Yes. What are you doing here?"

Tommy bent over and picked up a length of the long chain. He rattled the shiny links at her. "I'm one of the privileged guests. Can't you tell?"

"I don't understand. Nobody's supposed to be here. He promised I'd be alone. I don't want anybody here."

It was easy to comprehend the irritation coupled with anxiety in her tone. Tommy watched her place both hands firmly against the mattress and struggle to push herself farther up, before she collapsed back against the pillows behind her. She was having a difficult time of it, he noted. He dropped the length of chain back to the floor and stepped forward in a silent offer of help.

"No, don't." She glared up at him, the anger crossing her face quickly erased by a mask of determination. "Don't touch me. I can do it myself."

"Hey, fine. I was only trying to help. Don't bite my head off."

Tommy stepped back from the bed and slumped down in the chair a few feet away. He raised one leg and rested his unshackled ankle on his knee. Fingertips steepled under his chin, he contemplated the hostile young girl.

"You're Rebecca Burton, right?"

"How'd you know that?"

Tommy shrugged. He knew she didn't know him, didn't recognize him from school. Heck, nobody did. He was pretty much invisible there, too.

"We go to the same school. I remember you from the

drama club's play last spring. You were pretty good."

"Oh." A pink blush colored her cheeks. "Thanks."

An irritated frown marred her previously placid face. "Nobody's supposed to be here. He promised. I'm supposed to be by myself." She muttered the statement more to herself, evidently not expecting an answer. An undercurrent of anger threaded her words.

Not like I can answer her anyway, he thought. *I don't have a clue why I'm here either.*

"So, anyway, why'd you end up here? Did the nutjob grab you off the street, too?"

The girl looked at him with a puzzled expression. "What nutjob?"

"You know, the guy who carried you in here bundled up like a mummy. *That* nutjob."

Tommy watched her face closely and knew the moment she understood who he was talking about. She grinned.

"Oh, him. He's not a nut. He's okay. Actually he's helping me out. You know, tough times and all." Tommy watched as she raised her hand to brush back the fall of hair that swept across her cheek, her fingers pushing the wayward strands behind her ear.

"I just don't understand why you're here." Becca pointed to the chains. "None of this is the way it's supposed to be— the way he promised me. And don't call him that." She sniffed, a mulish look hardening her visage. "He's not crazy."

"Believe me, he's crazy. I didn't exactly shackle myself in this room, you know. I've been here a while. I'm not even sure how long it's been anymore."

The sound of a key being turned alerted him Steven was back. Steven walked in and pulled the door closed behind him. He noted Tommy's position before his eyes shifted to the bed. A smile lit his face when he saw the girl sitting up against the headboard, pillows supporting her back.

"Hello, baby girl." Steven's voice was filled with a wealth of love. Tommy was puzzled at the display. He really cared about Rebecca. Steven had shown more emotion in those few words than in all the time he'd been held hostage.

Tommy watched Steven approach the brass bedstead and seat himself on the edge of the mattress.

"You doing okay?" Steven's hand brushed gently at the bangs hanging across her forehead.

"I'm okay, I guess. Wasn't exactly expecting company, though, you know? What gives?"

"I know, baby. I'll explain it to you later, all right? It's a real long story." Steven smoothed down the blanket and picked up the girl's hand. Tommy watched it all, trying to piece together exactly what was going on. What was Steven's relationship with this girl? He seemed genuinely fond of her. If he cared about her, why was she a hostage, too?

"I wanted to check on you, see if you needed anything. I've got to go out for a bit."

"I'm fine. Woke up a few minutes ago and met Tommy." She glanced over at Tommy. He blushed and looked away. "There's only one thing I need anyway, and you've got it." She looked up at Steven, doubt clouding her eyes.

"You do have it, don't you?"

"Don't worry, sweetie, it's outside. I'll get it."

Tommy watched Steven pull open the door and reach for something just beyond his line of sight. Steven backed into the room, propelling a wheelchair through the open doorway. The rubber-shod wheels barely cleared the doorjambs.

Rolling the chair over next to the bed, Steven locked the handbrake into position.

The smile on the young girl's face left Tommy awestruck. She seemed positively thrilled at the sight of the chair.

Tommy tensed when Steven approached him. He remained seated in the chair he'd occupied throughout this entire bizarre conversation. He drew back as far as he could at Steven's approach. Steven leaned in close, his breath a whisper in his ear.

"Remember what I told you," Steven quietly uttered, running a solitary finger down the side of Tommy's face. "Touch a hair on her head, upset her in any way, and you're dead."

Steven walked back to the bed, bending to place a brief kiss on Rebecca's forehead before heading toward the door.

"Bye, sweetie. Be good."

Her eyes met Tommy's before she turned toward the door.

"I'm always good, Uncle Steven."

Chapter Six

Steven paced the floor in front of his kitchen countertop, back and forth, his mind reeling. *What have I done?*

He hadn't stopped to think things through the night he picked Tommy up by the side of the road. He'd fully intended to take him into town, to get his flat tire fixed.

As they drove, though, he started thinking about Becca. Pretty, sweet Becca. She was so alone now, she had nobody but him. Her parents, his sister and brother-in-law, had been killed instantly in a head-on collision six months earlier. Becca had been in the car with them, in the back seat, but had been thrown clear of the wreckage.

He remembered getting the call that horrific night from the doctors at the Baton Rouge hospital. He was the contact person listed on his sister's identification card, in case of emergency. He recalled the calm detached voice of the physician as he explained the facts, asking if he could come.

Becca lingered, clinging to life. The doctors, who hadn't expected her to make it, quoted him statistics and gave her less than a twenty percent chance of survival. But he knew she was a fighter.

He thought back to the moment he walked into the ICU room and saw her poor pitiful frame punctuated with all the tubes and machines helping her breathe, keeping her stable. Their incessant beeping, whirring, chirping sounds gave him pause, even as they gave him hope. She wasn't gone, and he wasn't letting go of her. She was all he had left, too.

They told him even if she did regain consciousness, Becca would most likely never be the same. The massive injuries to her spinal column and extensive head trauma made that nearly impossible. Her spinal injuries were irreparable. She'd be paralyzed from the waist down for the rest of her life.

The doctors told him taking her off life support would be the most humane thing, that he should "pull the plug" on his little angel. He couldn't. He would take care of her, no matter what.

He sat by her side for days, waiting, hoping and praying she would wake up.

Miracle of miracles, she finally opened those beautiful green eyes, so like her mother's, and smiled at him. He knew in his heart that she recognized him, that she wasn't brain damaged the way the doctors had feared. She was going to get better.

And she had. She had beaten all the odds and survived. That's when the real struggle began. They waited to tell Becca about her parents for several days, helping her regain her strength, to be strong enough to handle the news.

Standing at his sister's graveside, Steven had made her a solemn promise. When Becca awoke, he would do every-thing in his power to make sure she was taken care of for the rest of his life. Whatever it took. She would never want for anything.

Steven blinked, rousing from his memories, and glanced out the kitchen window. He saw the silhouette of the converted detached garage, set back behind the house. He had worked, day after day for the last three months, to get that apartment ready for Becca. He'd made sure it had everything she would need so she could feel self-sufficient. Independent.

When he visited her in the hospital, he told her all about it, using it as an inducement, a bribe, for her to work through the physical therapy sessions. He gave his word she would have everything she needed or wanted, if she would just get well.

Now, that garage apartment contained his living nightmare. Guilt tore at his guts every time his gaze locked on the converted concrete-and-brick structure. Every time he looked at it, it underscored to him what he had done. How many lives had he torn apart in his own selfishness? Good intentions or not, he had done the unspeakable, crossed a line from which there was no return.

Steven's abduction of Tommy hadn't been premeditated; it had been opportunistic. He needed a way to solve his problem and, at that precise moment, Tommy seemed like the perfect answer to his prayers.

Desperate times call for desperate measures. He hoped it was true, because there was no turning back now. The ball was in play and the game had begun. *God help us all.*

Chapter Seven

A mountain of paperwork waited for Max on his desk. Filing was a gargantuan task in his line of work, a part of the job he despised, so the stack climbed ever higher, threatening to topple. With the skillful hand of a man who had built more than his share of card houses, he slid a single sheet atop the pile. He was pressing his luck, knowing it could explode in a river of misaligned pages. Though it wobbled, the stack remained upright.

He'd thought to come in for a couple of hours, try to get his mind on to something other than his missing godson. So far they had nada, zero, nothing. His foot hit the magazines and newspapers piled high on the available floor space.

Taking a good look around his unkempt, overflowing office, he cringed. Something was going to have to be done and soon, before he was swallowed alive by junk. He plopped down in the leather chair behind his desk, bone-weary from both lack of sleep and worry. As a former cop, he knew what life on the streets was like. Degenerates and lowlifes populated the darker, seedier realms. He prayed Tommy hadn't fallen victim to somebody like that.

Theresa was trying to help, he'd give her that. He just didn't believe in all that crap about psychic phenomena. It was all B.S.

Leaning forward, Max turned on the laptop that sat in the midst of the clutter, keying into his favorite search engine as soon as his system booted up. With his unique two-fingered style, he typed in "psychic investigations," and literally hundreds of listings appeared. Were they all con artists, trying to make a buck, or was anyone legit, he wondered.

Clicking the mouse on the first one, he pulled up an article from a Missouri newspaper. It outlined how the police used a psychic to help in an investigation. The psychic investigator had given them several clues to the whereabouts of a missing woman, tips and suggestions that finally led to her rescue from a brutal ex-boyfriend, who'd tortured her for days.

The next link he clicked was an article by a noted celebrity paranormal investigator who specialized in debunking psychic phenomena to wide public acclaim. He'd proven several so-called psychics were not only charlatans but were bilking people out of huge sums of money in the process.

Well, he thought, *if there's one thing you can say about Theresa, she's never asked anybody for a dime, not for any reason.*

He scrolled through site after site, most of them no help at all. One caught his attention with the headline Psychic Abilities Linked to Traumatic Events.

The author of the piece claimed many of the psychics he'd interviewed, while varying in the levels of their abilities, showed a remarkable tendency to have suffered some traumatic event which triggered their "gift."

Closing down his browser, Max stood and crossed through the cluttered space to stare out the office window, pushing it open and letting in the noise and scents of the French Quarter. The bustling crowds at street level could be heard, laughing and joking as they went about their day, oblivious to the turmoil all around them. The smell of seafood, rich and spicy, filled the air. The enticing scent of freshly baked bread wafted his way, causing his stomach to rumble. He realized it had been a long time since he last ate and decided to grab a bite.

Locking things up tight, he took the steps two at a time heading for ground level. Briskly he walked the cobbled street with long, purposeful strides, as people stepped back to let him pass.

Stopping abruptly, Max found himself in front of Theresa's shop. He shook his head and started to turn away. It hadn't been his intention to come here. Still, he grasped the doorknob, turned it and entered the shop.

At the sound of the door opening, Theresa looked up from totaling the daily receipts. She'd been expecting Max to show up. The tension emanating from him earlier that morning at the Saunders's home had been a palpable living thing. On the drive back to town, he barely said a word, though his silence spoke volumes.

"Has there been any news about Tommy?"

"Not a damn thing."

As always, Max's presence dwarfed her shop, making everything seem small and insignificant. Though he tried to hide it, she could see the hint of despair in his eyes. Even with his mental shields in place, his body language was easy to read. She'd been studying him for years.

"Something will come up. Whoever took him will slip up and you'll catch him." Theresa felt the need to reassure Max. Or maybe it was herself she was trying to convince.

"We don't have time, though. The longer he's missing, the less likely we'll catch this sick bastard and get Tommy home safe." Stuffing both hands in his pockets, Max paced back and forth.

"Well, if you don't have any other news, why are you here?"

He barked out a short laugh. "Truthfully, I'm not sure. I was walking from my office, going to grab a bite, and somehow ended up in front of your place." Max smiled. "Want to get some dinner with me?"

Theresa's heart raced. Was Max asking her out? After the fiasco nine months earlier, she hadn't thought he'd ever talk to her again, much less want to see her socially. It was a start. Maybe they could make an attempt at mending their fractured friendship.

"I'd love to. Give me a minute to lock up these receipts and the deposit, and I'm yours." As soon as the words left her mouth, she cringed inwardly. *Very poor choice of words there, girl. Let's not open old wounds.*

Max sat down in the chair opposite hers, resting one booted foot atop his knee. "Do what you've got to do. I'm not in any rush." He leaned back, tilting the chair on to two legs, balancing precariously.

Locking the money and receipts in the wall safe, Theresa grimaced when she looked down at her attire. Not exactly going-out-on-the-town clothes. They were her usual working ensemble of loose unstructured blouse with a billowy, multicolored peasant skirt. Wearing the oversized clothing made her more comfortable around the public, and she shied away from clothes that exposed much skin or emphasized her figure.

Grabbing her purse and keys, she turned back to Max. "I'm ready whenever you are."

The chair thumped solidly against the gleaming wooden floor as Max stood with an easy, practiced motion, graceful and sexy at the same time. Sometimes just catching a glimpse of him made her desire rise. To have him here, alone with her, made Theresa's thoughts turn lustful. His long dark hair shone, catching the light, accentuating his steel-gray eyes. Her attraction to him was inevitable as the sun rising in the east each day.

"You in any particular mood?"

"What?" Her voice squeaked. He couldn't possibly know what she'd been thinking. Could he?

Max grinned, the corner of his mouth tugging up, a calculated gleam in his eyes. "Food. You in the mood for anything in particular?"

She thought for a minute. She was a sucker for seafood, and if he was offering a choice…

"Never mind, I know. Seafood it is."

"Am I that predictable?"

Max winked. "Nope, I just know what you like."

They walked to a cozy restaurant off Bourbon Street, a place frequented by regulars and tourists alike. Prices were reasonable and the food was superb.

Within minutes they were seated at a secluded table outside in the garden patio. The smells wafting up from the kitchen boasted an aroma of the finest ingredients and made ordering a chore. With so many choices, they finally settled on the special—a jambalaya with rice, a local blend of seafood, spicy and fragrant. Fresh-baked crusty French bread accompanied the meal, and Max ordered a bottle of white wine.

The busy streets of the French Quarter could be heard but the sounds were muted by the bougainvillea-covered wrought-iron fence and the wind whispering through the tree branches, creating a gentle breeze not too cool for the November evening.

They ate in companionable silence for a few minutes, enjoying the quality of the food and the company. Theresa's glance continually swept over Max.

He caught her looking at him, and a smile played around his full sexy lips. Theresa wondered if she'd ever feel those lips kissing hers again. She missed the tingling electric pulse she felt when his skin touched hers, the zing of awareness when his hands caressed her.

"I'm sorry I wasn't able to tell you anything more from

Tommy's room today. I'd hoped to get something, but sometimes it's like that, nothing cooperates."

Max leaned back in his chair, and pushed his plate away.

"Tell me about your psychic ability. I'd like to understand more about it."

Theresa hesitated before answering. She didn't like to talk about her gift. She didn't shun her abilities, but neither did she broadcast the fact she had them.

"Mostly what I have is called psychometric ability or psychometry. That's where I touch something, like Tommy's cell phone, and get an image or vision from it. It's not the full extent of my abilities, but it's probably my strongest."

★　　★　　★

"How long have you been able to do this? All your life?" Max studied her face. If he hadn't been watching for it, he wouldn't have noticed the slight flinch, the immediate blanking of her expression. After his research earlier in the day, he'd hoped not to see that reaction.

"Not all my life, no. It's not important."

"Why isn't it important? I'd think the longer you'd had your ability, the better you'd be with it."

Her cynical laugh surprised him. "That's probably true in most instances. I didn't always accept what I could do, fought it for a long, long time. So, you're right, I'm not nearly as strong as some other psychics are. Maybe you'd be better off going to consult with somebody else."

Max straightened in his chair. He knew he'd struck a nerve, but he didn't like where this was headed. "Are you backing out on me?"

"I just think you might be better off working with some-body stronger, more focused than I am." Picking up her purse, she stood and Max rose to his feet, as well.

"Look, I know the only reason you even came to ask for my help was because Remy practically forced you to. I think I've given you all the help I'm able to. You're on your own from here, Max. I really hope you find Tommy soon and that he's safe."

She turned and quickly walked away from the table. Max heard the faintest, "I'm sorry" drift back to him as she rushed out of the restaurant.

"I'm on my own now, huh?" Max signaled to the waiter for the check. He'd taken a calculated risk, pushing her that way. He knew she was hiding something and he wouldn't stop until he found out what.

Chapter Eight

Theresa knew it was going to be a bad day before she even opened her eyes. Her dinner with Max the night before played through her mind, highlighting in vivid detail all the reasons she'd tried to keep her distance. She recalled his probing questions. Walking away from both him and the case had been the right thing to do.

Swinging her legs around, she sat on the edge of the bed, glaring at the alarm clock. Sleep evaded her, and she'd spent the best part of the night watching the minutes turn to hours. Now she felt groggy and irritable, her eyes itchy and swollen. Damn him, anyway. Being a P.I. didn't mean he could snoop in her life.

It had been hard enough letting Max go nine months ago. Things had barely begun between them, at least in any romantic sense. A couple of dates. A few dinners. Physically they were compatible. More than compatible, she recalled, remembering the feel of his arms around her, the gentle yet persistent touch of his hands, caressing her willing, eager flesh.

It ended badly, though, with neither speaking to the other until he'd walked through the door of her shop looking for a missing teenager.

Last night emphasized they weren't cut out to be just friends. He was too curious, too inquisitive by nature. If he kept digging, asking questions, eventually he'd uncover things he didn't need to know. Things she prayed he would never find out.

It's best this way, she thought. *What he doesn't know can't hurt either of us.*

Quickly she dressed in her working garb, a long flowing skirt in a floral pattern bright with pinks, lavenders and blues. She topped this off with a loose tunic-style blouse in muted powder blue, belting the entire ensemble with a white crocheted belt. Fingering her hair into a long braid that hung down her back, she hurried downstairs to her shop.

She'd barely flipped the sign to Open and unlocked the door when Remy sauntered in, his step light. A quick grin curved his mouth.

She loved the way his smile lit up his entire face. It added depth to his ruggedly handsome countenance, giving him a charming, boyish quality most women found irresistible. Most women.

"Good morning, gorgeous." Hooking an arm around her waist, Remy pulled her close and dropped a quick kiss on her cheek.

This had grown into an almost daily routine between them. Remy worked the night shift and was usually just leaving the police station when she opened for the day. Most mornings, he dropped by for coffee and a quick chat before heading home for some well-earned rest.

"We still on for tonight?"

"Tonight?" She furrowed her brow, trying to remember if they'd had something special planned that she'd somehow forgotten.

"You didn't remember? Dammit, I should have kept my mouth shut."

Theresa raised her hand to her mouth, stunned that she had forgotten the date. For the first time in ten years, she'd actually forgotten what day it was.

"No, Remy, it's okay. Yes, we're definitely still on for tonight." They walked together into the kitchen, where their daily brew waited in the automatic coffee maker. Coffee was a big part of their morning routine.

"I think it's good you finally forgot our 'anniversary'. Any particular reason though?"

She felt the heat rise in her cheeks at his question. He knew her so well he could practically read her like a book.

"I, uh, went out to dinner with Max last night."

Remy choked on the coffee he'd just swallowed, struggling to catch his breath. "Max? You and Max went out to dinner? Together? Like on a date?"

"No, not like on a date. We just went out to talk about the case."

"Uh huh, right. That's why there are dark circles under your eyes, and you forgot about our annual celebration. Just talking business," he teased, his tone light and singsong.

Swatting a hand at him, Theresa quipped, "Shut up, Remy. It *was* just business. That's all it can ever be with Max and I. You know that."

Remy sobered quickly. "I know. I wish things were different. If I had a time machine and could go back and change the past…"

"No, no changing the past. If things were different, then I'd never have met you. I wouldn't change that for anything. You're way too important to me."

Remy grabbed her and pulled her close in his embrace, squeezing her tightly against his chest. "Me too, babe, me too. I love you, you know."

"Love you, too, Remy."

At the sound of a throat clearing behind them, she and Remy sprang apart like guilty teenagers. Glancing over her shoulder, she grimaced at Max's expression. Disapproval radiated off him in waves. *How did he get in without that damn bell ringing, again?*

"Morning, Max. Coffee?" At his brusque nod, she grabbed another mug from the cabinet and filled it. Theresa handed it to him black and steaming, pretending the two brothers sharing morning coffee with her was nothing out of the ordinary.

She knew he'd overheard her declaration to Remy. She wasn't ashamed of proclaiming her feelings for him. They'd been best friends for ten years. He was the closest thing to a brother she'd ever had, and she did love him. But, she wasn't *in love* with him.

That emotion belonged solely to Max, and had for more years than she liked to count.

Max never understood the bond between her and Remy, he probably never would. He'd mentioned it on more than one occasion. He even once accused them of being lovers.

"What brings you by, Max?" she asked.

Good. Nice and casual, friendly.

"We're working on a case, remember?"

"No, we're not. I quit last night. Remember?" Heavy sarcasm laced Theresa's words.

"Actually, what you said was I should try to find somebody with more experience. Then you stalked off before I had time to say anything at all."

"And from that you couldn't tell I'm not working for you anymore? Get a clue, Max."

"There's no reason to bring someone else in at this point. You know all the pertinent information. It would take too much time to bring somebody else in and get them up to speed." He hesitated. Max stood stone-faced, hands on hips but Theresa read the anger in his rigid posture. "You've actually been helpful on a few things. You were dead-on about where Tommy's cell phone was located. You had me stop at the exact spot."

"And why couldn't you have acknowledged that fact at the time? Wait, I know. Max can't admit the psychic might have gotten one right." Theresa stood toe-to-toe with Max. She jabbed him in the chest with her index finger, to make sure her point came across. "I'm not working on this with you anymore. Get that straight right now. I hope you find Tommy, I really do. But I can't do this."

Abruptly turning away from him, she glanced at Remy before bolting from the kitchen in a headlong dash to escape to the refuge of her shop.

Max started after her, but Remy caught his arm, shaking his head.

"Let her be. I don't know what went on last night—that's your business—but don't push her on this, okay?"

"Dammit, I'm not trying to push her, but right now she's the only chance I've got to find Tommy. As much as I don't believe in this crap, she's been right. I need her, Remy." Max ran a hand through his already tousled hair, pushing the strands off his forehead, only to have them fall back into their former place.

Remy took a good close look at his brother, taking in his pale appearance, the dark circles under his eyes and the haunted expression in them.

"I understand, but you've got to give her some space right now. This is hard for her." He waited a moment for Max to calm down. "She worked on a case with me, a bad one. About three years ago, a four-year-old girl went missing. The parents were frantic. Everybody feared the worst. The whole community turned out looking for that little girl. Hell, I even spent my off time searching for her."

Max nodded. "Yeah, I remember hearing about the case."

"Then you remember it didn't have a very happy ending. They found the child in the neighbor's covered pool, drowned. What wasn't released to the press is the fact Theresa was the one who told us where to find her."

Remy stood and walked across the kitchen area, leaning his hip against the countertop. Grabbing the carafe, he refilled his empty cup. He closed his eyes for a moment before continuing. "I'm the one who came to her and demanded her help. The department didn't know I was doing it. I brought a photo and a sweater of the little girl's. I can still picture that sweater. It was blue with pink and white flowers all around the neck and down the front." He rubbed a hand along his jaw.

"I practically begged her to help me. Theresa wouldn't touch the picture, wouldn't even look at it. She turned so pale, it was like all the blood had drained from her face. She started shaking, saying she didn't want to touch it. I pried her fingers apart, shoved the damn sweater into her hands. Made her hold it." Remy's voice caught, breaking slightly as he fought for control.

"Remember what you saw on the side of the road, how she kind of goes *away?* That day, she actually stopped breathing. The moment she touched the sweater, her eyes rolled back in her head, she fell backwards." Remy put his cup down and grasped the back of a chair, his focus intent on Max.

"Understand me, Max. *She. Quit. Breathing.*" Remy remembered frantically yanking the sweater out of Theresa's hands and starting CPR. "When she finally took a gasping breath and opened her eyes, I read it in her expression. She knew that little girl was dead."

"Jesus, Remy. I had no idea. Why the hell did you send me to her if you knew something like that might happen? Forget it. I'll find another way. She's out."

Theresa's voice sounded from behind them, strong and determined. "Forget what I said earlier. I'm going to find

Tommy."

She moved around to stand next to Remy, facing Max. Her gaze met his directly, not a waver or falter. "And when I do, we're done. I don't ever want to see you again."

Chapter Nine

Tommy watched Becca as she struggled to move from the bed to the wheelchair parked beside her bed. She'd worked at shifting her weight across the single bed for the past few minutes until she was finally at the edge.

It was agonizing to watch, but he didn't attempt to help her. When he'd tried, moments earlier, she snapped at him. He knew she wasn't really angry with him; it was frustration.

Her limp, motionless legs hung over the side of the bed. Unshed tears filled her eyes. When her fist hit the mattress, a muffled explosion of sound caused him to jump.

"You can do this." She stated this with conviction, speaking to herself. "You've been transferring for weeks now. This isn't any different than before."

She lifted her head, her defiant glare fixed on Tommy. "It's the height of the bed that's thrown me. The one at the rehab clinic was a regulation-height hospital bed. This one's not the same." Her words tried to justify her actions, even though they were unnecessary.

She braced her hands on the armrests of the chair as she stood, placing her full weight on her stiffened arms, swung her body around and dropped down hard onto the seat.

Yes, he mentally cheered. She'd done it.

Manually lowering the footrests, she lifted each leg, one at a time, placing her feet on the metal supports. She released the brake, easing the chair forward. Only a few feet away, she rolled to an abrupt stop.

"Can you please move that out of the way?" she grumbled, pointing to the length of chain coiled on the floor, directly in her path.

Grimacing, Tommy stood and lifted the silver links out of the way. "Sure thing, Your Highness."

"Don't be such a sarcastic ass." She snorted in a distinctly unladylike fashion, and rolled forward toward the bathroom.

Tommy chuckled at her retort, and heard the distinct click of the lock on the bathroom door. Moments later the sound of the shower running could be heard.

Her strength amazed him, not just physically but emotionally. Although she hadn't told him much, from the few snippets he'd heard between her and "Uncle Steven," he'd pieced together some of what had transpired over the last several months. "She's adjusting better than I would have," he mumbled aloud.

He still didn't have a clue why Steven had snatched him. He hadn't asked for ransom or tried anything funny, either. Tommy had been more than prepared to fight with every ounce of strength he had, but it hadn't been necessary. Things just didn't add up.

The sound of water shutting off alerted him that Becca would be out soon. He got a kick out of arguing with her. She was feisty and rose to the bait so easily. But he wasn't here to make friends, was he? Didn't matter how nice she was, or whether or not he felt sorry for her. As far as he was concerned, she was on the side of the enemy, and he'd need to watch his back around her.

Long moments passed but finally the bathroom door unlocked and swung inward slowly with a thump, followed by muttered cursing. It opened all the way, and Becca rolled out, fully dressed with a towel wrapped around her damp hair. Wheeling herself into the kitchenette, she opened the mini fridge and pulled out a can of soda, placing it in her lap, before pivoting and wheeling forward until she was back in the living space.

Tommy moved the shiny length of chain before she asked, allowing her more mobility, limited though it was. She rolled to a stop by the CD player and placed her soda can on the table beside it. Sifting through a stack of disks, she selected one, sliding it from its case, and slipped it into the player. Soon the sounds of a duet by George Strait and Alan Jackson filled the air.

"I wouldn't have taken you for a country music lover," Tommy said, walking over to perch on the lone chair situated beside the end table. "Figured you'd go more for that New Age, girly stuff."

"Shows what you know. I have very eclectic taste. Right now, I just happen to be in the mood for country music." Picking up her soda, she popped the top, taking a ladylike sip.

"Would you like a glass for that? I mean, a paper cup, since we don't have any glasses?"

"If I'd wanted a cup, I'd have gotten it myself." A flush

of pink flooded her cheeks. "Thanks for the offer though."

"No problem. You need anything else?"

"Yes. I need to know what the heck is going on around here."

Tommy slouched farther down in the chair, lifting his chained leg to rest atop the opposite knee. He ran both hands through his short hair, scrubbing at it so hard, it stood on end.

"I've been asking myself that question from the minute I woke up here. Your uncle Steven won't tell me why he took me." His hands played with the silver links running from the manacle, letting the slack play through his hands, back and forth.

"I had a flat tire on the way home from my job. Started walking back toward New Orleans, going to find a filling station and get it fixed. Steven stopped and offered me a lift. I said, sure, why not? He was a friend, does work for my folks all the time."

"But why are you here, like this?" Becca was actually listening to him this time, with interest.

"Don't know. Steven said he needed to stop off at home then he'd take me to get the tire fixed. When we got to his house, he invited me in to have something to drink. Next thing I remember, I'm waking up in my new home away from home." Tommy gestured toward the four walls encompassing them. "I can't get a straight answer out of him. For days, he barely spoke to me. Just brought food on those lousy paper plates and crappy paper cups."

"He was supposed to be fixing this place up for me, my

own refuge for when I got out of rehab. Nobody else was supposed to be here. Heck, nobody else was even supposed to know I was here."

"See, that's what's so strange. He never said a word about you. Just showed up with you bundled in those blankets, carried you in and laid you down on the bed. Threatened me, ordered me not to touch you, or he'd kill me. Hell, I didn't even know who you were. My first thought was that he'd kidnapped somebody else and they'd be stuck here like me."

"Well, we are both stuck here in our own way, aren't we? Neither one of us has our freedom." Becca's voice held a hint of sadness.

"I remember hearing about you being hurt a while back. What exactly happened, if you don't mind my asking?"

Becca glanced down at her lap, at her useless legs, before returning his stare.

"Long story made short, my parents and I were in a car accident six months ago. They were the lucky ones." Her voice cracked slightly. "They were both killed immediately. I was in a coma for a while. When I finally woke up, Uncle Steven was there. The nurses told me he'd been there every day, from the first day I was brought in."

"So he's taken responsibility for you?"

"Pretty much. That's why I can't believe he did something like this. Why kidnap you?"

Tommy stood, the chain making a jangling noise as it hit the cement floor.

"If you figure it out, let me know, 'cause I've racked my

brain and I can't come up with any logical reason. I mean, my God, who in their right mind chains somebody up in their garage? You ask me, he's just friggin' crazy."

He walked across the room, as far away from Becca as he could get, leaned back against the wall and slid down to sit on the floor. Pulling his knees up, he rested his elbows on them and placed his hands over his eyes, effectively shutting her out.

Softly, so softly he almost didn't hear, Becca whispered, "That's what I'm afraid of. That he really is crazy."

Max walked the few blocks back to his office, his mind replaying the things Remy had said. He didn't want to hurt Theresa. Now he understood how traumatic this psychic ability of hers could be, the physical toll it took on her. He wanted her out.

Worse though were those final words before he left her place. *I never want to see you again.* Those simple words were like a knife stabbing his heart. The relationship between them had been pretty rocky, true, but there had been some good times, too.

He almost hadn't asked her out at first, not wanting to come between Theresa and his brother. Then he finally convinced himself they might have a chance.

When they first started dating, it had been so sweet. She had opened up like a blooming flower, glowing and coming alive before his eyes. Then he ruined it with harsh words and even harsher accusations. He cringed at the taunts he'd thrown at her.

He deliberately sabotaged any chance at a relationship because he'd been afraid. What he felt for her scared him, made him want things he had no business wanting. Max had nothing to offer a decent woman like Theresa, so he'd done what he felt was best and pushed her away.

Regret filled him now at the loss of what could have been. Upstairs, in his office, he was greeted by the same scene he saw day after day. Old, care-worn furniture, good quality pieces but showing their age. Filing cabinets buried under mounds of paper waiting to be put in their proper place.

He bent and picked up the mail scattered on the floor, leafing through it as he sat in his leather chair, propping his feet up on the edge of the desk. Separating the envelopes, he catalogued each one: bill, bill, advertisement, junk, junk. At the next one, he froze.

The upper left corner showed the embossed address of the Shreveport District Attorney's office. Tossing the rest of the mail down on the desktop, he opened the center drawer and grabbed his letter opener. His fingers trembled slightly as he slid the sharp blade along the envelope's top edge then pulled out the folded sheets.

He braced himself, expecting the worst. As he skimmed the letter, his shoulders slumped. Relief flooded through him. He'd been completely exonerated on all counts. The guilty party had been caught, clearing him and his former partner of all suspicion. The Shreveport Police Department even offered him his job back, reinstated at full pay and benefits, if he wanted to return to the force.

Fat chance.

He and his partner, Joe, had worked a huge drug bust. A large portion of the drugs and weapons somehow managed to disappear from the evidence room. When the stuff turned up on the streets again, they were accused of stealing it to sell for profit. They were both suspended, and the investigation had dragged on forever. With the insurmountable evidence growing, he and Joe had been not-too-subtly encouraged to resign.

Joe was the first to quit. He had a family to protect. Eventually, Max did the same, and moved back home to New Orleans.

Two long years and he finally had a resolution. Max knew he should feel angry, but he didn't. He'd been disillusioned by the whole fiasco. He loved being a cop, loved everything about it. Because of one stupid man's greed, two lives had been irrevocably changed.

The knowledge it was finally over, even after two long years, should mean something, yet he still felt empty. *It's probably the case, Tommy being missing.* He'd find time to feel good when Tommy was home safe and sound.

"Man, who are you kidding?" He strode over to the window and leaned against the sill, staring down at the people walking along the sidewalk. He wasn't thinking about Tommy right now, he was thinking about Theresa. Again. More and more she filled his thoughts, a daily distraction Max couldn't afford.

His mind returned to the research he'd done on psychics. Theresa admitted she hadn't had her abilities all her life and it made him wonder what kind of trauma she must have gone through to bring her latent talents forward.

Worst-case scenarios raced through his mind, each more horrible than the last. He knew from past experience just how intolerably cruel man could be to his fellow man. Anyone working in law enforcement encountered it on a daily basis. The thought she had undergone something so bad she couldn't even speak about it made him sick.

It ate at him, the not knowing. The knowledge she was pushing him away, just as he pushed her away nine months before. Guilt was a jagged blade, cutting deep. It threatened to push him over the edge.

He knew he made a mistake a year ago, intentionally hurting her with cruel words and unfair accusations. The vast gulf between them ate at his conscience. Keeping his distance from Theresa wasn't working. Just being back around her this short time, asking her to work on Tommy's case, brought back all those old feelings. How much he wanted her, desired to be with her. Their attraction hadn't faded. If anything, it was stronger than ever.

Keeping secrets got them nowhere. He needed to rebuild the trust he'd shattered, to mend a few broken bridges in the process. And he was going to do it tonight.

Theresa and Remy strolled arm-in-arm through the teeming crowd of tourists. They'd just finished a leisurely dinner, their appetites replete. Theresa smiled as they passed a couple standing in front of one of the shops, the man down on bended knee, obviously proposing. She hoped they'd be happy together, knowing they basically had a fifty-fifty chance of making it for the long haul.

Once home, she unlocked the back door and reached for the light switch, illuminating the kitchen's gleaming appliances and spotless countertops.

Wordlessly, Remy reached into an upper cabinet, pulling out two wine glasses, while she went to the refrigerator for the bottle of wine he'd placed there before they'd gone to dinner. Tonight was their standing ritual, a rite they'd performed for the last ten years. It was a bittersweet celebration, the anniversary of a day that had changed both their lives.

Theresa smiled, handing him the wine before sitting in her favorite chair at the kitchen table. He worked the corkscrew, deftly opening the bottle to fill each glass.

"Here's to another year together." As she spoke, she lifted her glass in a salute, her eyes never leaving his. A look passed between them, further words unnecessary.

"To my best friend. May we have many more years together like this, celebrating life, love and happiness." Remy's words echoed her thoughts. She knew he understood better than anybody else how important his friendship was to her.

Smiling, she leaned forward slightly and they lightly clinked glasses before sipping the wine.

"It's hard to believe another year has passed. I think it's finally getting easier. At least it seems that way." Theresa felt the truth in her statement.

"I'm glad. I know neither of us will ever forget, but as

time passes, maybe it'll become a faded memory, and you can be happy."

Theresa shook her head, eyes lowered. *Here he goes again.* "Remy, it's not going to happen. Not now and not ever. Max and I had our chance once, but it wasn't meant to be."

A sharp rap on the back door sent her attention flying to the inset panes of glass. Her heart fluttered when she saw Max through the window. She started to stand but Remy beat her to it, opening the back door.

"Hey, bro, whatcha doing here?" Curiosity laced Remy's words.

"I needed to talk to Theresa—about Tommy's case."

"This late at night? Couldn't it wait till morning?"

Max eyed his brother, his gaze shifting from Remy to the two wine glasses on the table, before stopping on Theresa. His heartbeat kicked up a notch. Dressed in a simple black sheath dress, her blond hair piled in a loose, attractive style on the back of her head, Theresa looked stunning. He swallowed past the lump in his throat. A burning pain centered in the midst of his chest, his heart thumping wildly. Had he interrupted something? Max realized the gnawing, wrenching feeling in the pit of his stomach was jealousy, eating at him at the thought of Remy and Theresa together. "Look, if I'm interrupting something important, I'm sorry." *No, I'm not, not really.*

"Yeah, actually, bro, you are. Theresa and I are— celebrating. Our anniversary." Remy pressed his lips together tightly, unable to hide his amusement. "Maybe you should come back tomorrow. Late tomorrow. We're probably going to be up all night." Lifting his hand to cover the smile he could no longer contain, he gave Theresa a conspiratorial wink.

"No, I don't think it can wait."

Theresa stepped forward. "What is it that's so important?"

An awkward silence followed her question, as Max struggled to come up with a plausible reason for being there. Although he'd come to press her for more information about the trauma in her past, to share his own secret with her, he didn't want to push in front of his brother.

"When we talked at dinner last night, about your psychic abilities—powers, whatever you call it—you said you hadn't had them all your life. When exactly did you develop your gift?"

Theresa was stunned that he would come right out and ask. She thought she'd have more time, with him subtly trying to determine the cause. Then again, she should have known better. While Max was a whole lot of things, subtle wasn't one of them.

"It doesn't matter when I developed my abilities. I have them and they can help with your investigation. That's the only thing that's important."

"Look, you've been right on a couple of things so far, I'll grant you that. But you haven't given me anything concrete, something tangible I can wrap my hands around. Anybody with some skill at deductive reasoning could probably tell me the same things and they'd never claim to be psychic."

Max prowled forward, his loose-limbed stride bringing him closer, stopping bare inches in front of her.

"I'm a skeptic. Make me believe you'll be more help than hindrance in this case."

Theresa narrowed her eyes, her lips tightening to rein in her aggravation. She was so tired of his disbelief. No matter what she said or did, it always came back to proof.

"Probably makes you a good detective, but a lousy choice of a friend." Her finger stabbed at his chest again. This time her hand brushed up against something in his jacket pocket. The vibrations emanating from it were overwhelming. Focusing, she absorbed the energy flow and channeled it.

She stared into his steely-gray eyes.

"Okay, Mr. Skeptic. There's a letter in your pocket. It's a very important letter—something you've been waiting on for a long, long time." Max slowly nodded before folding his arms across his chest, his stance rigid.

"Will you believe me if I tell you what I can about the letter? You know I haven't seen it. Will that convince you that I'm not a phony?"

"It sure as hell would go a long way toward your credibility."

"Fine. Have a seat."

This ought to be good, Max thought. He pulled out a chair

and eased his long frame onto it. Remy followed suit. Theresa remained standing, her hip against the tiled countertop, her stance relaxed, but her expression unreadable. Her face was blank except for her eyes. They gleamed green in the kitchen light, shooting sparks, all directed at Max.

Without a word he reached into his pocket, pulling out the letter. Removing it from its envelope so she couldn't see the return address, he hesitated a split second before handing the folded letter to Theresa. Clasping it in both hands, she threaded the sheets between her fingers, angling it first one way and then another, staring at the stark whiteness of the paper. Finally after what seemed like an eternity to Max, she began to speak.

"Two years ago you quit your job on the Shreveport Police Department and came back to New Orleans. You told everybody you were burned out, needed a change. Not true, though, was it, Max?"

Max continued to stare at Theresa, close-lipped. He nodded again.

"There were some problems there. You were being investigated—missing evidence, wasn't it? You and your partner were accused of stealing drugs and weapons from lockup and selling them."

Max felt blind-sided, stunned by the accuracy of her declaration. His jaw went slack before he quickly snapped it shut. Through gritted teeth he growled, "How the hell did you know that? I didn't tell anybody."

"Dammit, you didn't even tell me." Hurt laced Remy's

voice.

Pointing to the letter still clasped between her hands, Max said, "Go ahead. Open it. Read it." Theresa unfolded the pages and started reading. She stopped once, glancing at Remy before continuing to the end. Max watched her, searching for a reaction to its contents. *Nothing.*

Carefully refolding the letter, she handed it to Max. He stuffed it back inside the envelope before shoving it into his pocket. Vindication should have tasted sweet. It didn't. All he felt was a remote sense of loss for what might have been.

"They've offered you your old job back?" Theresa's quiet voice belied the anger still filling her eyes.

"Are you going to take it?" Remy asked quietly.

Max shook his head. He stood and walked to stand by the sink.

"No, I'm not. I'm glad my record has been cleared, don't get me wrong, but I like being in charge of my life. I'm staying right here."

★　★　★

Inside, Theresa rejoiced. He was staying. For every part of her that never wanted to see him again, for every self-preserving instinct of flight, there was another part that wanted to be near him, to fight for what they could have.

"Was that enough to convince you, Max, or do you need further proof?"

"There's no way you could have known any of that information about me. Like Remy said, I've never told a soul, not even my baby brother."

Relieved she wouldn't have to prove herself to him anymore, she let herself relax.

"How did you get so much just from touching that letter?" Max's words were more curious than accusing. "But not from Tommy's phone or something from his room?"

"It doesn't work like that. If it did, I'd be a multimillionaire living the good life." *Not really, but hey it sounded good.*

"I can't control what I *see* or *don't see.* I will either get vibrations or images from an object or dead space—nothing at all. Sometimes I'll get a feeling before I even touch an object—if there's a darkness associated with it—but that's rare." Theresa ran a hand across her forehead, brushing wisps of hair back.

"My abilities aren't something I can call up on a whim. They just are. I'm not sure where they'll take me, but I'm done running from them. Believe me or don't, that's your choice."

"Hey, I already said I believe you—now." Max's voice filled the kitchen, his belief a panacea to Theresa's frazzled psyche. *Maybe he'll drop it.* His next words dispelled that illusion.

"The reason I came over here tonight was to ask you about your ability. I've been reading up on psychics and I keep running into the same information. That's why I asked you if you'd had your gift all your life. I want to know when it started."

Theresa's eyes widened and she looked to Remy. Her breathing sped up. Max's words chilled her to her very soul. Remy reached across the table, clasped her hand and gave it a quick squeeze.

"All the experts I've read state when a psychic gift came on later in life, usually around adolescence, it was triggered by a trauma in the psychic's life."

Stepping forward, Max stood in front of Theresa and tilted her chin up with one finger, meeting her eyes. "If we're going to work together, you've got to trust me. What happened to you? What's your secret?"

Chapter Ten

Theresa stared at Max, trying to gauge how much she should tell him. Remy sat across from her and vigorously shook his head, his intent clear, not wanting her to dredge up her hurtful past.

"Remy, go home. I need to talk to Max."

"Hell, no. He doesn't need to know a damn thing. It's none of his business," he shot back.

Remy glared at his brother, his gaze filled with anger at Max for forcing the issue. Max had no idea what demons he'd raised. Only Remy shared those memories with her—nightmares from that horrific day—the source of a ten-year friendship which had stood the ravages of hell.

Theresa pushed her chair back and skirted the table, placing her hands on Remy's tense shoulders. She placed a kiss on the top of his head, inhaling the clean crisp scent she always associated with him. "I'll call you later, I promise. I need to speak with Max. If we're going to continue working together, he needs to know. Everything."

Max remained silent through it all, arms crossed, feet planted. From his rigid stance, Theresa could clearly tell he wasn't at all happy at how protective of her his brother was. Her relationship with Remy surpassed Max's understanding.

But then, most people hadn't been through the kind of trauma she and Remy had. Dark, violent memories forged an unbreakable link that withstood the passing years.

Remy stood and hugged Theresa. Standing at the back door, he shot a warning look at Max, his frown stating "don't you dare hurt her."

Max stood still, his feet braced apart, his hands lightly skimming the back of one of her kitchen chairs. To the casual observer, he appeared calm and collected, even at ease. She probably knew him better than most. She'd loved him for a long, long time. Calm and collected in no way described him right now.

"Sit down." Theresa took another glass from the cabinet and carried it back to the table. Reaching across, she lifted the bottle and filled the glass nearly to the top before setting it in front of Max. She inhaled a steadying breath, ran her trembling fingers along her skirt, then lifted her gaze to his.

"Is this so bad I'm going to need that?" Max questioned, slowly running a finger around the rim of the glass, his gray eyes flashing with banked fire.

"You may not need yours, but I certainly need mine." Lifting her glass in a mocking salute, she gulped the red wine. She needed its fortifying strength. After all, she was preparing to tell him all the things she kept hidden down in the deep, dark corners of her soul. The ones that grab you by the throat when you least expect it. *Like tonight.*

She lifted her trembling right hand and brushed a lock of hair back, tucking it behind her right ear before looking at Max. "Some people are born psychic. Others have a latent gift which never comes out. Occasional flashes or hints of intuition, but nothing solid. Others have their abilities thrust upon them, brought on by a physical or emotional trauma." She paused for a moment to gather her thoughts. *Why is this so much harder than I thought it would be?*

Max reached across the table to cup Theresa's cheek gently. His fingertips lightly skimmed her jaw and butterflies tickled the inside of her stomach, whispery light, matching the feelings his touch evoked as he stroked her skin.

"Whatever you tell me, it can't be as bad as all the things I've imagined since last night." She straightened at the sound of his voice, drawing back farther against her chair, away from his distracting touch. *Does he know how just the touch of his hand affects me? Dear God, I hope not.*

"We've know each other over ten years. Why now? Why is it so important for you to know every minute detail of my life?"

"Damned if I know," Max muttered. "I just—I can't explain it—but I have to know."

Theresa stood, needing to place some distance between her and Max. Just a few feet separated them, but it may as well have been miles. Not only in distance but in time.

She remembered their first date. How special he made her feel with something as simple as dinner and a movie. They even held hands when he walked her home. At the door, he leaned in and kissed her tenderly. His lips so sweet, so…

Arms twined around her, startling her from her musing. They snaked around her waist, drawing Theresa against a rock-hard chest. Leaning her head back, she rested it against Max's shoulder, savoring the feel of his hands against her stomach. Even through her clothes, she felt the heat of his touch.

"Do you remember how good we were together?" Max nuzzled her neck, his whispered words causing an ache deep inside her chest. His lips caressed her skin. She felt the rasp of his tongue as he licked a slow path along her jaw. Instinctively she turned her face toward him and his lips captured hers in a searing kiss. Spinning in his embrace, Theresa wrapped her arms around his neck, pulling him in closer as she opened her lips to his. A battle of tongues and teeth and lips. Rising on her toes, Theresa strained to get closer. *God, how I've missed this, missed him.*

Breaking the kiss, Theresa inhaled deeply, hands trembling. She took a step back, cupping the side of Max's face before dropping her hands to her sides, balling them into fists. She ached to go on, pull him back in and continue kissing him forever. That was part of the problem. Kisses led to caresses. While she loved the feel of his hands on her bare skin, remembering it in vivid detail nearly every night, that was as far as it had ever gone. *As far as it can ever go.*

"Damn. Not again." The confusion in Max's voice brought her gaze up to meet his.

"What?"

"Do I repel you in some way?" His question startled Theresa.

"It's not you. It's never been you, Max. It's…me."

"Then why? Every time I touch you, kiss you, you pull

back." Frustration etched Max's countenance but not anger. Theresa was surprised there wasn't anger.

"Max, has Remy ever told you how he and I met?" With a wave of her hand she indicated he sit before taking the chair across from him.

Max's brow wrinkled then he shook his head. "Now that you ask, no, I don't think he ever told me. I guess I just assumed it was at school."

"Funny, Remy and I did go to the same school. I was a year behind him. We never met. Not until I was fifteen, almost sixteen. I was really shy in high school. Somebody like Remy, so outgoing, the life of the party, he wouldn't have looked twice at a wallflower like me."

She looked at the wine glass in front of her, not wanting to meet Max's intent stare. "Aren't you curious about what Remy and I were 'celebrating' tonight? We were celebrating the tenth anniversary of our first meeting. After all, it was a momentous occasion. It's the day he saved my life. And my sanity."

Max's head jerked up. "What the hell's that supposed to mean? While this psychic BS may make you certifiable, as far as I'm concerned you're one of the sanest people I know."

Theresa laughed mockingly at that. "You wouldn't have thought so if you'd seen me then."

She picked up her wine and took another sip. "Ten years ago tonight, Remy saved my life. Literally. He found me out by Marshall Road, lying in the bushes."

Max tensed as if anticipating what she was going to say.

"I was walking home from school because my dad had to

work late, a double-shift, and he couldn't pick me up like he usually did. I heard a vehicle coming so I moved over to give it room to pass. A pickup truck slowed down and stopped. I recognized the two boys inside—they both went to my school but were several grades ahead, seniors. They were laughing and joking, the way jocks did. They asked if I'd like a ride. To be honest, I felt a little flattered they would stop for me. I wasn't stupid, just incredibly naïve. I didn't know either one of them except by sight, so I said no. Unfortunately, they weren't taking no for an answer."

"Oh, God. Theresa." The expression on Max's handsome face was one she had hoped never to see directed at her. The pity, the shock at what had happened, became a ruthless reality.

"Please, don't interrupt or I'll never be able to tell it all." She looked down at her hands and realized she was fidgeting with the rings she wore, a habit she had outgrown many years ago.

"One of them circled around behind me and grabbed my arms before I knew what he was doing. They dragged me into the bed of their truck. Marshall Road was hardly ever used back then. You rarely saw a car go down there once every couple hours."

Theresa forced herself to remain calm, ignoring the gut-wrenching, acid-filled pain dredging up these memories brought. It hurt more than she'd believed possible. But she continued anyway.

"I fought. God, believe me I fought, but it was two against one. Fighting was useless. *They raped me.* They tore my clothes, not caring about the damage. Their fingernails dug into my skin, leaving red marks and scratches that didn't go away for ages. One of them slapped me. He seemed to enjoy the pain he inflicted." She shuddered at the memory, the pain as real today as it had been ten years before. "He laughed."

Reaching for her glass, she took another sip, relieved her hand was steady. She couldn't look at Max. Not yet.

"They laughed the entire time. It seemed to go on forever. I didn't make it easy for them, though. They hit me several times, slaps, a few punches. I think at one point I even passed out."

She continued, letting her words sink in. "When they were finally finished, they carried me and my shredded clothes back to the side of the road, a few feet back into the overgrowth and dumped me in the bushes like garbage."

She watched Max pinch the bridge of his nose between shaking fingers, and knew she had to finish.

"I'm not sure how much time passed after they left. It seemed like hours. I know it started to get dark, and I think I was more afraid of being there in the dark than of anything else. All I could think was my dad was going to get home from work soon and I wouldn't have his supper on the table. But I couldn't move."

As the words tumbled forth, she closed her eyes, partially to recall things with better clarity, but mostly not to see Max's face as he listened to this shame-filled portion of her past.

"What I didn't know was that, in the initial struggle, I

dropped my book bag on the ground beside the street. For God knows what reason, Remy had decided to ride home down Marshall Road that day. Divine intervention, maybe. He saw my bag and stopped to see who it belonged to. He told me later he heard a sound, an indistinct whimpering. Being the Boy Scout that he is, he had to investigate." Now she looked directly at Max as she spoke. "Thank God he did. I was lying there in the weeds, bruised, battered and bleeding from everything they had done."

"Stop. Don't say any more," Max interrupted, but Theresa placed her hand on top of his, silencing him.

"No, let me finish. This all needs to come out. Remy was amazing. Truly amazing. Even back then, being only seventeen, he was astonishingly mature for his age. He was riding his bike and there was no way he could hold me and pedal. So he took off his jacket, wrapped it around me and told me to stay hidden. About ten minutes later he was back with a car.

"He wanted to take me to the hospital, to the emergency room, and have them call the police. But I was so scared, Max. I wouldn't let him. I fought him even though he was only trying to help. I scratched and hit him, not letting him touch me. Finally, he just sat down with me in the grass, there at the side of the road and held me while I cried and raged and cursed God for what had happened."

She reached up and wiped at her eyes and the tears slowly trickling down her cheeks.

"He finally convinced me to get in the car and brought me back to my dad's house. By the time we got there, I was practically catatonic. I couldn't talk, couldn't think. Everything seemed to just shut down. He helped get me into the house. My father wasn't due home for another hour. I was a total mess. My clothes were in shreds. I was covered from head to toe with scrapes, scratches and bruises, to say nothing of the dirt, grass and Lord knows what else from being left on the side of the road.

"Max, you need to understand, I was helpless at this point. Traumatized, abused. My mind had shut down. But Remy's didn't. He was my rock. He stripped off my clothes and held me under the shower while he was fully clothed, and he cleaned me up as though I were an infant. That's how helpless I was."

"He can be a rock when he needs to." Max's voice brought Theresa back to the present and out of the vicious pictures playing in her head.

"Once he cleaned me as best as he could, he took me out of the shower and bandaged all my cuts. He got me fresh clothes and dressed me as though he had been doing it all his life. Then he put me in bed and pulled up the covers, all the way up to my chin. Through all this, I hadn't said a word. I had shut down."

Theresa met Max's gaze directly as she spoke. "Remy stayed with me until it was time for my father to come home. He even made dinner for my dad, so he wouldn't know anything was wrong. I made him promise me, while we were still on Marshall Road, he would never tell anybody about what happened. I think if he hadn't given me that promise, I'd probably have died there by the side of the road.

That or I'd have killed myself.

"Somehow I managed to hide what happened from my father. I called in sick to school for the next couple of days, stayed home and tried to cope with everything. Remy came by the next day after school and checked up on me. He came by the next day, and the next. He always asked me the same question. Who were they? He wanted names."

"Damn right he wanted names. I do, too. The sons of bitches have to pay."

Chapter Eleven

Max could barely contain the rage roiling through him. *Damn them to hell!* Theresa stood in front of him shaking her head.

"No. You don't need their names. I never gave them to Remy, either. Nobody knows who they are but me. You can't make them pay for what they did."

"Like hell I can't! Just watch me," Max insisted.

Theresa walked over to the sink, resting both hands against the rim, her head down. She turned slowly around. "They've already paid."

"How?" Max's deep rumble filled the room.

"Less than six months after it happened to me, they raped another girl from our school. She was braver than me. She reported it to the police. They were arrested, convicted and sent to prison. They're still there."

"Good. I hope they rot in prison."

A broken laugh escaped Theresa before she bit back the sound. "In that we're in total agreement."

Max stood directly in front of Theresa, placing one finger under her chin, tilting her face upward. The light from the overhead kitchen fixture revealed the trail of tears across her pale cheeks. Cupping her face in both hands, he gently wiped away the tears with his thumbs, whisking away the moisture. He placed a tender kiss against her forehead.

"Baby, words can't express how sorry I am for what you've been through. I wish you had been able to confide in me sooner."

"Max, I—"

"No," Max interrupted. "I understand why you couldn't. At least, I'm trying to." He reached forward and grasped her hand, giving it a tug. Stepping behind her he gave her shoulders a soft nudge, pointing her toward the stairs leading to her apartment. Twisting around, Theresa looked back at him before starting up. Max followed right behind her.

At the top of the stairs, he stopped when Theresa paused in the doorway. He'd been in her apartment before, many times. It was a homey, comfortable place. The décor suited her to a T. But he wasn't really seeing it now, he was solely focused on Theresa. Empathetic he wasn't but he knew she was hurting. He just wasn't sure what he could do to help.

Nudging her forward again, he directed her to the sofa. Hands on her shoulders, he guided her back onto the cushions. He could read the stunned, somewhat distant look in her eyes, on her face. Walking to the bathroom, he grabbed a washcloth and dampened it with warm water. Back in the living room, Theresa sat where he'd left her, motionless.

He sat down beside her, using the edge of the damp cloth to gently wash away the tear stains. Her big green eyes, the look in them, tore at his heart. *I can't stand to see her like this.*

Leaning back, his arms wrapped around Theresa, drawing her into his embrace. He rested his chin on the top of her head, smiling when she snuggled in closer.

"So, the bastards are in prison?" Theresa stiffened slightly at Max's quiet question before relaxing back against his chest. He felt her slight nod against his chin where it rested atop her curls. He inhaled deeply, drawing in the scent that was uniquely Theresa's.

"Yes. They were convicted of first-degree rape. They're still serving their sentences."

"So are you, though, aren't you?" Max realized the truth in his words even as he said them. Theresa was locked in a prison within herself as surely as those men who had raped her were locked in 8x10 cells.

"What?"

"You're punishing yourself for something that isn't your fault. You couldn't stop them. You fought with everything a young girl could. Don't let them have that much power over you now."

Theresa drew back to stare at him. *How did he know?*

Max pulled her close again, and she rested her head against his chest. She could hear the rapid beat of his heart, feel the rise and fall of his chest with each breath. In his arms she felt…safe. More than that. She felt at home.

"Yeah, I guess I've been letting it define who I am," she replied.

"Tell me what happened afterwards," Max's compassionate voice murmured. She couldn't hear any accusation or demand in his tone, just a willingness to listen.

"About a week after everything happened, I went back to school trying to act as though everything was fine. After all, nobody knew. Except them. And Remy. But I felt everybody watching me, whispering. I convinced myself they all knew what happened and maybe felt I deserved it."

Max started to speak again but Theresa patted his chest, silencing him, gently rubbing her index finger over the smooth cotton of his T-shirt. He closed his mouth, but gave her hand a reassuring squeeze.

"I know. Nobody deserves to be treated like that. But I was so young and naïve. I thought maybe I'd done something to make them think I wasn't a good girl. I know differently now. Those bastards didn't think anything about me. All they thought about was themselves and the power they had over one foolish girl.

"Anyway, I hadn't walked down Marshall Road again since that day. But something made me go there. It was like I was drawn there, compelled in a way I had never felt before. I ended up back at the spot where they'd attacked me. I hadn't even realized where I was walking until I got there. I stood there, looking around and thinking about the two of them. Hating them but mostly hating myself."

God, it's so hard to tell him this. I never wanted him to know. She brushed the thoughts aside, focusing. Drawing in a deep breath, slowly exhaling, she counted to three before continuing.

"All I could think was that I didn't want to go on. I

wanted everything to just stop. The thoughts, the memories, but mostly the dreams. They were the worst part. I kept having these horrible, vividly frightening dreams. Not about the rape but about things that happened to other people I knew.

"That was the really scary part. I didn't know anything about psychics or extrasensory perception back then. I just knew something was different. *I was different.* I would touch something belonging to somebody else and get these pictures in my head. Nobody else had those kinds of dreams. Dreams about other people being hurt, being killed. *I wanted the nightmares to stop.*"

"Baby, I'm so sorry. More than I can tell you. But I'll say it again. It was not your fault."

With Max tenderly cradling her in his arms, holding her and running a hand slowly up and down her back, Theresa felt safe in a way she hadn't for ten long years.

"Everything was too much for me to handle. The rape, the nightmares, the images. I truly didn't think I could handle it anymore." Theresa's voice was barely above a whisper. "I wanted to kill myself."

Max cursed, erupting in a string of expletives. Theresa knew they weren't directed at her but couldn't stop the involuntary flinch. Max's arms tightened about her, pulling her close again.

"Obviously, I didn't do it, but I thought about it. Seriously considered ending everything." Staring up into Max's eyes, Theresa sighed and relaxed against his chest again.

"It was Remy, you know? He became my anchor. Every

day, rain or shine, he was there, spending time with me so I wasn't alone." Theresa pictured it in her mind, remembering the young boy on the verge of becoming a man taking on the responsibility of caring for her, somebody he didn't really know.

"I'm not sure if he sensed in some way what I was thinking about doing, but for whatever reason, he was always there." Theresa chuckled. "My dad used to call him The Fly. Said he was always hanging around me like a fly drawn to honey. Papa would grab him around the shoulders and point him toward the door and say, 'Shoo, fly, shoo.'" Theresa smiled at the fond memory.

"Remy never said a word about any of this. Not to me and I know not to *Maman*. If he had she'd have grabbed her shotgun and hunted the bastards down like dogs." Theresa snuggled closer to Max, and his fingers absently threaded through her curls, wrapping one around his finger.

"I'm sure she would have."

"Probably would do it today if I tell her. Want me to sic her on them?" Max chuckled, the rumbling in his chest strangely soothing to Theresa. A distant echo of thunder followed his words, the deep sound mirroring Theresa's emotions, the ache in her heart.

"I'm glad you trusted me with this."

Placing a finger under her chin, Max tilted her head back slightly, his eyes filled with so much tenderness Theresa's breath caught in her throat. She searched his face, hoping to see some sign of what he felt. Leaning forward, his eyes still wide open, Max's lips lightly brushed hers, sending a charge of electricity racing through her entire body. It was always the same whenever Max kissed her. Her body responded immediately, one half of a whole, subconsciously searching for its mate.

Theresa pulled back, reluctantly breaking their kiss. She pushed a fall of hair over her shoulder.

"Sounds like a storm's coming. Are you going to be okay here alone? I can stay or I can have Remy come back if you'd rather be with him?" The concern in Max's voice tugged at her soul, reawakening feelings she thought long buried.

Theresa ran her fingers lightly across Max's lips, a brief yet poignant motion. She then lowered them, clasping her hands in her lap. *I can't do this. I can't let him get too close. I can't let him break my heart—again.*

Inching back and away from the warmth and security of Max's embrace, Theresa put precious space between them. The span was more than mere inches. A wide gulf stretched before her, as though she stood at the edge of a precipice. One wrong move, one misstep, and she'd never recover. Giving a mental shake, she distanced herself from him, physically and psychologically. With the revelations she shared with him tonight, it was all too much, too soon.

She noted the puzzled expression on his face, but he remained silent. He reached for her hand and she drew back before he touched her.

"Theresa—" Max whispered.

She interrupted him before he could continue. "I'm okay. It's been a long night. How about I give you a call in the morning and we'll talk about the case? We'll both be able to think more clearly then."

Looking at Theresa once more, Max slowly turned and walked out, closing the door behind him.

Theresa made sure he was gone before covering her face and letting the tears flow, knowing the revelations of this night would irrevocably change the relationship between them. She only wished she knew if it would be for the better or for the worse.

Chapter Twelve

Steven looked at the row of pill bottles lined up like little soldiers, marching from tallest to shortest on the coffee table in front of him. So many prescriptions. Pills he had to take throughout the day, every day, in a vain attempt to control the pain, make the blinding headaches tolerable. The agony grew worse with each passing day.

Shifting forward on the sofa, he reached for each bottle, emptying out the correct dosage. He gathered the multicolored tablets and capsules together. Chugging the glass of water, he washed them down. The urge to gag rose but he fought it.

Staring at the empty glass in his hand, fingers clenched around it, he hurled it across the room, watching it crash against the wall, shattering into a million glittering shards. The light reflected off the broken pieces, twinkling and mocking him with their brilliance.

Head in his hands, his body bowed in pain. *Please, please make it stop. I can't take it anymore.*

The blackouts were getting worse. He lost longer periods of time with each episode. He'd come out of one of the spells not knowing where he was or how he got there. Worse, he had no idea what he'd done during those missing hours.

Each day he prayed he wouldn't do something like he'd done with Tommy. The boy haunted his nightmares. He knew the anguish and despair he was putting Tommy's parents through. After all they had done for him, keeping him employed year-round, both with his lawn service as well as his handyman business—this was how he repaid them. He'd stolen their only child.

I had no choice. Something had to be done, actions taken. In one of his delusional moments, it had seemed so right. Had made complete sense. He needed somebody to take care of Becca. His sweet, helpless Becca. Life had been so unfair to her, causing her to lose everything: her parents, the use of her legs and, very nearly, her life.

Now she was going to lose him, too. That's what all the pills were for. They bought him a little more time, maybe a few short weeks.

Brain cancer. That's what the doctors had told him. Inoperable. They could try radiation, they said, maybe chemotherapy, but when all was said and done, it was a death sentence. His death sentence.

Walking to the kitchen, he grabbed the broom and dustpan. He needed to clean up the broken glass, while he was still thinking clearly. Through the window above the sink, his gaze caught on the detached garage behind his house.

It isn't fair. I should be here to take care of Becca. Instead, she was going to go through another loss, another tragedy in her life.

Steven had always been pretty much a loner. His only family had been his sister and Becca. His life centered around his job and building up his business. While he had a few friends, none were close enough to burden with the responsibility of a disabled teenage girl.

This was his reason, his justification for taking Tommy. Tommy was a good kid—almost an adult. His parents had raised him right. He'd grown into a responsible young man. Steven was counting on that.

He'd put them together, close confinement. His twisted logic assured him that they would develop a strong bond.

He knew his reasoning skills were skewed now, his thinking not always sane, but he carried the hope that once he was gone, Tommy would take care of Becca.

Scrubbing his hands over his face, he carried the broom into the living room. They just needed more time together. He'd seen the way Tommy's eyes stared at the wheelchair, the gleaming metal, its padded seat and chrome spokes. Steven watched him closely, knowing immediately when the realization had sunk in that the chair was Becca's.

Sweeping up the broken glass, careful to ensure he got all the shards, he disposed of the fragments in the kitchen trashcan then gathered the prescription bottles, stacking them back into the cupboard and out of sight. When they were put away, they weren't a constant reminder of the miniscule amount of time he had left. He could pretend everything was normal, that life was a good, happy place.

First things first, though. He knew what he had to do next. Walking back to the living room, Steven sat at the old oak desk, the one he'd received from a client in payment for a job. Pulling open the middle drawer, he lifted out blank paper and a pen. When this was over, when the end finally came, he knew there would be unanswered questions.

Laying the sheets on the desktop, he began to write.

Max pulled into the driveway of his mother's home. The headlights illuminated the lone silhouette of a man seated on the front porch swing, effortlessly rocking the wooden seat back and forth. Through the open car window, he heard the whooshing sounds the chains made as the old swing slowly swung to and fro, each movement propelling it an equal measured distance. A flash of lightning lit the porch followed by a rousing clap of thunder.

He knew Remy waited for him, anticipating his reaction to the truth Theresa revealed such a short time earlier. It explained so much, yet Max wished with all his heart he didn't know. If he could, he'd make it all go away as though it never happened.

Turning off the engine, he stepped out of the car and walked the familiar rutted pathway to the porch. He inhaled deeply, catching the scent of the wild honeysuckle that grew around the front and side railings, climbing wildly in uncontrolled abandon. His mother was forever fighting to keep it contained. She threatened each year to hack it all out or pull it up by the roots, but everybody knew she'd never do it. She loved the scent of honeysuckle in the evenings; part and parcel of the memories of quieter times spent gathered together on this porch.

Max strode over to where Remy sat and reached out his

hand. Remy slapped a cold bottle of beer into it. *Too bad it's not a whiskey.* "I could use something a hell of a lot stronger than a beer." Max twisted the cap off.

He took a strong pull on the longneck, the icy cold beer sliding down his throat. Max tilted back his head and closed his eyes, sighing audibly.

"I don't know how you've lived with this for so long, Remy. Right now, I'm not sure if I should hug you or beat the crap out of you." Max looked directly at his brother, trying to gauge him. Usually, Remy was as easy to read as an open book, but not tonight. In the softened glow reflected from the front porch fixture, Remy's face was closed and drawn.

"Dammit, Max. Do you have any idea what it's been like for her? She's had a hard life, but she's become a strong, determined woman because of it. Now you've dredged it all up again to satisfy some morbid curiosity. That's intolerable."

Max felt the pulsating anger radiating off his brother. He knew that anger wasn't really directed at him. It was directed at the two bastards who committed such a heinous act ten years earlier.

"Did it help, Max?" Remy hissed. "Did having Theresa bare her soul in all its excruciating detail get you one step closer to finding Tommy? Hell, no. All it's done is muddy up the waters even more." Running a hand across his face, Remy met Max's gaze directly. "Do I need to go back there, Max? Is she okay? Really okay?" Setting his bottle on the porch railing, he started down the steps. "Forget it, I'm going anyway."

"No, don't." Max's words caused Remy to pause. "She needs to be alone right now. Give her tonight, and call her in the morning."

Leaning back on to the railing, Max hitched his hip on to the wooden fencing and rubbed a hand over his neck, massaging at the tense, stiff muscles there.

"Jesus, Remy, how could you keep this to yourself all these years?" Max slammed his fist into the post beside him, wincing as the skin scraped along his knuckles, blood oozing.

"It was her decision, her choice. I honored her wishes. They've gotten away with it for ten years, and I haven't been able to do a damn thing about it."

Max laid his hand on his brother's shoulder, squeezing. He knew Remy didn't know who raped Theresa; she'd told him that. Even though Remy was her best friend, her confidant, she had shared the whole truth only with him.

By trusting him, she opened his heart to feelings much deeper than friendship. Max cared about Theresa because of who she was; her strength and honesty, and the integrity she had shown through all the time he'd known her.

He'd seen the real Theresa tonight, and he planned to get closer to her than ever before.

Chapter Thirteen

He finally knew everything. All her past, her pain.

Theresa had never wanted Max to find out what happened to her so long ago, to see the pity in his eyes. But she'd also seen a compassion she hadn't expected. He'd been hurt, angry, but he also understood.

She remembered his anger when she told him about the assault, his immediate demand for names. He'd have gone straight out and hunted them down, she knew, if it were possible.

A smile fluttered around the corners of her lips, a touch of sadness filling her. Max seemed to think her will to survive was amazing. That she was a strong, worthwhile person. Maybe, just maybe, if enough time passed, she might be able to think so, too.

Theresa sat at the table situated in the center of her shop, her hands folded atop the multicolored scarves, and closed her eyes.

She focused, letting her subconscious self free, and concentrated on Tommy, sorting through the evidence gathered so far. There was just so little to go on.

Feeling a familiar pull, she watched the patterns and shapes evolving, searching them for clues. At first everything was gray. A rough-textured, porous-appearing mass. She sharpened the edges, feeling as though she were looking at blocks in a specific pattern. *Concentrate,* she thought.

"Cinderblocks?" Puzzled, she moved deeper, but all she saw was more gray, though slightly different in appearance. A shinier gray, with a smoother textured. It had more of a polished cast to it. *Maybe concrete or cement?*

The gentle jingling bell sounded. Theresa looked up as Remy quietly closed the door behind him. Without a word, she went to him and was enfolded in a tight embrace.

"I'd give anything for you not to have relived that again." As he spoke, Remy held her secure in his arms, his touch a comforting blanket spreading the warmth of his love and friendship through her.

"After all these years, it feels good it's finally out. I think Max understands now why our relationship is so special. Why you're special to me."

She brushed her lips against Remy's cheek, thankful and amazed this kind soul was such an integral part of her life.

"Let's grab some coffee. I know you've got some made by now." Taking her hand, Remy half-pulled and half-pushed her into the kitchen, and headed straight for the overhead cabinets where she kept her coffee mugs. He knew his way around almost as well as she did.

He grabbed two mismatched, brightly colored mugs and filled them to the brim with the coffee she brewed earlier. He added a dollop of cream and a teaspoon of sugar to hers, the way he knew she liked it. His was black with two sugars.

"Coffee should be like sin," Remy said, grinning. "Black

as your soul and temptingly sweet to make it worthwhile."

He placed both mugs on the table and pulled the chair out for Theresa, before he swung the opposite chair around and straddled it. Picking up his coffee, she watched him inhale the rich aroma of the special chicory blend. He took a long swallow, a blissful expression crossing his face.

"Ah, *cherie,* you always make the best coffee. I swear I'm tempted to move in here, just so I can get it every morning."

Theresa laughed. Remy said that every time. He loved her coffee and never failed to show his appreciation.

"Sorry. It's only a one-bedroom place, and I don't share well."

Remy's eyes squinted slightly at her words. "Yeah, I know. We're both too independent to ever be able to live together. Wouldn't last a week." He waggled his eyebrows at her, doing a great Groucho Marx impersonation. "Would be kinda fun while it lasted, though, wouldn't it?"

Theresa laughed.

"Max was really pissed by the time he got back to the house last night. Thought he might actually hit me for keeping things from him."

Theresa lowered her head, her eyes not meeting Remy's. She hoped he didn't notice the dark circles beneath her eyes she'd seen in the bathroom mirror that morning. She had to deal with Max herself. Knowing that didn't make things any easier, though.

Theresa raised her head up and brushed back her hair, letting it spill down her back. She blinked away the unshed tears.

"When are the two of you going to stop this? You fight so hard to keep him at a distance. Every time he tries to get close, you push him away."

She hadn't realized he knew.

Remy knelt in front of Theresa and took her hands in his. "What? Did you think you were hiding it from me?"

"Oh, God, Remy," Theresa whispered, "there's no chance of any kind of a relationship with us." Tears flowed silently down her cheeks, her voice cracking on a broken sob.

"Honey, there's always a chance. There's been something brewing between the two of you for years. Trust me, he's fighting this just as hard as you are."

"You don't understand. I'm in love with Max. But there's no chance of a future with him. There's no chance of a future with anyone."

Theresa pulled her hands free from his and wiped at her tears. She looked into the eyes of her dearest friend, trying to quell the riotous emotions swirling inside her. Last night had been cathartic in its own way, but there were still things nobody knew, things she hadn't even told Remy. Maybe now was the time. No more hiding.

"It seems like all I'm doing lately is crying. I'm stronger than this, dammit." She straightened her shoulders, drawing on her inner strength. She paused for a moment as she gathered her fragile composure.

"I can't be with a man physically. I've tried." She watched his eyes widen, grateful when he remained silent.

"A few years after the assault, after I graduated from high school, I went away for a few months. I had that internship with a newspaper in Baton Rouge. My father was so excited, and so was I. It gave me a chance to get away. To be independent."

Remy nodded. "I remember. I'd just finished my first year of college and was home for a break."

"Yeah. I met somebody at the paper, a fellow intern. He was a year or two older than me. We got to know each other, went out a couple of times. I felt the time was right, that I was ready to have a deeper relationship. Shoot, I was ready to have sex. I was eighteen, and it's not as if I was a virgin."

Remy straightened as Theresa rose from her chair, walking around it and grasping its back. Her knuckles whitened with the strength of her hold.

"We went to his place after dinner one night. I had it all planned out. I even had condoms in my purse, to make sure everything was safe."

She glanced at Remy but couldn't quite meet his eyes. This was embarrassing. They'd talked about everything over the years, but the topic rarely turned to sex. It wasn't taboo, they just seemed to avoid the subject.

"We talked for a bit, kissed. That part was nice. Okay, it was better than nice. We were having a wonderful time." Theresa paused a moment, embarrassed. "I-I couldn't do it."

Remy interrupted, "Honey, it was probably still too fresh, too painful. You can't let this scar your entire life."

"It wasn't just that one time, though. Remember John, the guy I dated a few years back?" Remy nodded, his lips pursed in a sour expression. Theresa knew he never really cared for John when they dated.

"I tried to be intimate with him, too. I thought we would be good together. We'd taken our time. I cared about him. Same thing happened."

"Just because it happened then doesn't mean it will happen with Max. You weren't in love with those idiots. It'll be different with him."

"I'm not willing to take that chance. Not now, not ever. He deserves so much more than what I can give him." Theresa choked back tears.

And I won't get my heart broken by him again. I can't.

"That's just plain BS and you know it." Remy turned an accusatory glare on her, and she flinched. "Don't give up on Max. He's not going to be happy without you."

The vehemence in his tone surprised her.

"Don't look so shocked. Max is fighting his feelings tooth and nail, but it's a losing battle. He wants you. You want him. Go see a shrink, a priest, do something. Don't give up on your future."

The back door flung open, slamming against the opposite wall. Max stalked into the room, his sinewy muscles rippling beneath a tailored navy-blue shirt. Tight jeans encased muscular thighs. With each step closer, Theresa felt the invisible flames of lust flickering within her. Her desire for him never diminished, it grew stronger every day. He stared at them, a question in his eyes.

"Theresa." Remy pulled her attention away from Max. "Remember what I said. If it's what you want, fight for it." With that, he sauntered through the back door, leaving her alone with Max.

Chapter Fourteen

"Did I interrupt something?" Max drawled out his question, scrutinizing her face. His lips curled upward slightly as he arched his brow, mildly amused. He knew he had interrupted and didn't care.

"Not a thing. Remy stopped by for his morning coffee, just like he always does." Theresa lifted the carafe. "Would you like a cup?"

"Sure," he replied. "It's been a long night. I could use it." *One of the longest nights of my life,* Max thought. He'd replayed Theresa's agonized confession over and over, the thunderstorm outside a fitting orchestration to accompany each painful word. Seeing her this morning, remembering what she had gone through and how he'd once treated her made him feel like the biggest jackass alive. Even knowing about her past and the devastating psychological toll it had taken on her, he still wanted her more than any other woman he'd ever met.

"Has something happened?" Theresa's voice came out a bare whisper. She cleared her throat and waited for his response.

"I got a call from a friend who works just across the river in Mississippi. They raided a chop shop and broke up a stolen car ring. He said they found a Suzuki there, which they thought was unusual. They tracked the VIN number back to David Saunders. It might be Tommy's bike. I'm on my way there now to check it out."

He paused for a moment and took a sip of the coffee. "I wondered if you'd like to go with me. Maybe you can get something off it, if it is Tommy's bike."

"Really?"

The corner of Max's lips curled at the surprise in her voice. "Yeah, really. You've been pretty accurate so far, it's worth a shot. We have to leave pretty soon, if we want to get there and back today."

"I think I can get Maggie to cover for me. Give me a couple of minutes to call her and we can be on the road."

Max watched Theresa pick up the phone and dial her friend. He took in her gently rounded hips under the long loose folds of her skirt. Even the bagginess of her clothing couldn't fully hide her distinctly feminine shape. As much as she tried, the shapeless clothing always seemed to encourage men to stare at her. He couldn't blame them. She was a gorgeous woman.

"She'll be here in just a couple minutes. I'll go change and we can be on our way." Turning, she made a mad dash up the stairs.

"Great." Sounding rougher than he had meant, Max winced. He hadn't slept a wink the night before. The events Theresa described scrolled through his mind like a movie, the images blurred and shady, but clear enough to give a detailed picture of the traumatic events she suffered at such a vulnerable time in her life.

He fought his attraction to her, too. The more he was around her, the more he wanted her. He'd finally admitted that much. Max found himself watching her whenever they were in the same room, especially when he thought no one could see. It was becoming a desperate obsession, his need to see her, to touch her. He knew he couldn't. She didn't feel that way about him, not anymore. Any romantic feelings she may have had toward him died nine months ago.

When Theresa came back into the kitchen, his eyes widened at her attire. Whenever he'd seen her recently, it was in or around her shop, wearing the loose, billowy skirts and blouses that complemented her New Age surroundings. Now, she was dressed in a light blue form-fitting cardigan, the first few buttons undone, displaying a lace-edged camisole underneath. And jeans. Tight, molded-to-her-backside-like-a-second-skin blue jeans.

He swallowed, easing the lump in his throat. Sure, he'd seen her in jeans before, several times, but he didn't remember them hugging her backside in quite that butt-cupping way. They molded to her curves, outlining them in just the right way to make him reconsider taking her along. His erection grew tighter, harder. He hoped he'd be able to walk out of her kitchen without her noticing.

"Let's ride." Max took her arm and led her out to his pickup.

Theresa dipped her head to hide her smile as she climbed

into the cab of Max's truck. *That worked well,* she thought. She debated all of two seconds on what to wear, Remy's words echoing in her mind. She reached into her closet, pulled out the jeans and her brand-new cardigan and changed into them before she could talk herself out of it.

She knew she looked good in the jeans, and the blue of the sweater complimented her blond hair. Normally she would have pulled it back into a ponytail or a braid, but today she left it long and flowing. Max liked it loose, cascading in a cloud over her shoulders and down her back. It had been a long time since she'd done anything to it, other than a quick trim to keep it healthy, so the shiny length reached almost to her hips now.

Max glanced in her direction, taking in her appearance as they drove in silence, the low cadence of the radio the only noise in the truck's cabin. She saw him look at her once again then quickly turn his eyes back to the highway.

"How long do you think it'll take to get there?" She shifted in her seat, angling toward Max. He drove like he did everything else, competently yet with an impatient, reckless edge.

"Couple of hours, probably. Three tops. It's a fairly rural town, so I'm surprised they made a connection to the case this fast."

"What will it mean if it really is Tommy's bike?"

"I'm not sure yet." Theresa could see the crinkles at the corners of his eyes as he contemplated her question.

"If it was stolen, he'd have called his folks, or the police. If he was stranded someplace, he has an emergency credit card. He's even got my number, he knows he can call me day or night and I'll help him." Max's gaze met hers again, before reverting his attention to the road.

"He didn't run away. He wouldn't do that to his parents. Plus, he knows I'd find him."

"In my vision, he got into that vehicle voluntarily. There was something wrong with his bike." Theresa pondered that. "When the police found it at the chop shop, was there anything wrong with it?"

"Brad didn't say. As soon as he noted the VIN number matched the one reported on the missing person data, he called it in."

Max slowed his speed as the traffic became heavier and more congested on the outskirts of a town similar to numerous ones they had passed through since leaving New Orleans an hour earlier.

"Thanks for coming with me." Max's voice sounded strained.

"I want to help find him. I know how important he is to you."

Max reached across the bench seat and grasped her hand, raising it to his lips and pressed a soft kiss to it. Theresa's heart skittered at the surge of desire that raced through her, but said nothing. She was more than happy to let Max hold her hand while he drove. Somehow it felt right.

Max and Theresa ran into some unexpected delays due to road construction, the bane of Louisiana traffic. It was close to two o'clock before they reached the rural Mississippi police station. Walking through the glass-fronted entrance and the obligatory metal detector, they were led back to meet with Max's contact and friend, Sergeant Brad Cohen. Tall, lean-hipped and whipcord thin, he wore his blond hair long, as if he hadn't had time for a haircut recently. Fine lines around his eyes, accented by dark circles, gave silent testimony to long hours on the job.

Brad stood to greet them when they were ushered into the interview room.

"Hey, Max, good to see you again. Ma'am." Max made introductions, noting the way Brad's gaze swept over Theresa in obvious appreciation, and his temper began to simmer. *Calm down and don't be an ass. You haven't got any right to feel possessive about her.*

Once they were seated, Brad filled in the details of the arrest. As with everything else in this case, there weren't enough facts to be of much help. "One of the perps arrested said he bought the bike from an old guy. The man told him the bike belonged to his son, who'd been killed. They don't usually take motorbikes—too hard to fence—but he got it so cheap, he didn't ask a lot of questions."

"I want to talk to him," Max growled.

"Sorry, man, no can do. He's lawyered up just like the rest of the group, and won't say another word."

Max rose from his seat and prowled the available space, which in such a cramped room wasn't much.

"Just a couple minutes. He can even have his lawyer present. I need *something*, maybe a description of the guy he got the bike from."

"I've tried, Max. I talked to him and his lawyer. I explained about the missing kid. He won't budge. He's too afraid his ass is gonna fry for this mess. He's been arrested so many times this may be the icing on the cake that gets him put away for a long time."

Brad stood and braced his hands on Max's shoulders, stopping his relentless pacing. "I'm sorry. I even had the chief lean on the lawyer, but it's a no go. We can't force him to talk."

Max ran a hand through his hair, exhaled deeply and nodded. "I know. I figured that might be the case, but I had to try."

He glanced over at Theresa and met her steady gaze before turning back to Brad. "Can I at least see the bike, man? I'd recognize it if I saw it."

"Give me a couple minutes. I'll see what I can do." Brad walked out of the room, the door whooshing shut behind him. Theresa moved to stand in front of Max. She reached down and clasped his hand in hers firmly, without speaking.

He looked deep into her eyes. Pulling his hand free, he reached around and drew her close. A slight tremor in his hands betrayed his reaction to her touch. Her breasts brushed against his shirt, causing a spark of awareness to spring to life inside him. Max stilled, feeling her trembling response. He ran his fingers through the silky length of her hair and watched it slide down her back to where the glossy mass ended at her hips. His hand rested lightly on the small of her back, his look daring her to object.

She stroked the side of his cheek, her fingertips stopping at his lips. He lowered his head toward hers, his eyes open and aware of her every movement.

The opening door startled them apart, causing Theresa to nervously smooth down the front of her sweater, while Max retreated a step. Brad grinned at the scene but refrained from commenting. "Chief says you can take a look at the bike, but it stays in the evidence lockup. I'll show you where it is."

"Theresa goes with us." Max's tone brooked no argument.

Brad shrugged. "Come on, then, but we've gotta make it quick. This was a big bust for our town and the press is all over it."

They followed Brad to the evidence lockup and filled out the multiple forms necessary to view the bike. Finally, after what seemed like an eternity, they were led to the Suzuki. Max knew right away it was Tommy's, even without checking the VIN number. There was no license plate, but it really wasn't necessary. His gut and the familiar scratch in the gleaming black paint by the headlamp told him it was Tommy's bike.

"It's his." His head whipped around at Theresa's quiet voice. She stood only inches away. She held a hand out, skimming over the surface, a hairsbreadth from the cool metallic sheen. His breath caught as she moved. She circled the bike, still not touching it, her hand hovering just above its frame.

She gave a broken laugh, her voice catching at the end.

"I'm almost afraid to touch it. I want so badly to find him, but…I'm scared. Of what I might see."

Her hand slid along the leather seat of the Suzuki, and Max felt as though her fingers were sliding along his skin. Her fingertips circled the handlebars. He watched her curl her hands around the leather grip, squeezing lightly. Her eyelids drifted closed, shielding her eyes from the light. Long moments passed as he waited, giving her time to read the bike. *Dear God,* he prayed, *let her see something.*

Theresa waited for the familiar feeling to kick in. There was nothing. She placed both hands on the metal-covered engine. No psychic vibrations. No sense of Tommy.

She faced Max. He stood and watched her, his face expressionless. She knew he was afraid to hope.

She reached up and grasped the front tire and felt the sponginess, the rubber giving under her fingertips. *Flat tire.*

Stepping back, she dropped her hands to her sides and closed her eyes. She focused her energy and attempted to pinpoint a focus—to help her psychometric gift flare to life. Nothing happened.

"I'm sorry, Max. I'm not getting anything." She watched the glimmer of hope in his eyes die, leaving their gray depths bleak and empty.

Chapter Fifteen

After leaving the police station, Max and Theresa drove in silence. Max had spoken with Brad alone while she waited in the truck. She knew he needed those few minutes to himself. He hadn't let it show, but he was devastated she'd been unable to find anything new. Even with his inherent skepticism, she knew something inside him wanted her to prove him wrong, to find Tommy. *You've disappointed him.*

Max's voice broke into her thoughts. "It's been a long day. Feel like getting something to eat?"

"Sure, sounds good."

"There's a little place about fifteen miles from here. It has terrific seafood."

Theresa's stomach grumbled audibly at his words. She loved seafood. All of it—shrimp, crawfish, snapper, mussels—you name it, she'd eat it.

"Absolutely." She grinned at Max. "I'm always willing to make a detour for good seafood."

Max smiled. "Seafood it is."

A few more miles down the road they took an exit off the highway heading south. After about twenty minutes, he pulled the truck into a hole-in-the-wall place. It wasn't much to look at. Built like an old-fashioned log cabin, weathered and worn, it had seen better days. Family-style picnic tables lined up row after row, most of them filled with happily eating customers.

Max shoved the truck's gear into park and loosened his seatbelt. At the dubious look on Theresa's face, he burst out laughing.

"Come on. The food's terrific and the fresh air will stimulate your appetite." Coming around the front of the truck, he pulled open her door and thrust out his elbow. "Madame, your table awaits."

Laughing, she placed her hand on his elbow and walked with him toward the benches. He found them a place to sit and went to the window to place their order. When he returned, Theresa quirked one brow at him in question.

"It's a surprise. Trust me, you'll love it." They chatted for the few minutes it took their order to be ready. Superficial, mundane conversation. Small talk about the weather, anything and everything to keep their minds off the fact Tommy was still missing.

A burly overweight man with a shaggy beard called out their number. Max motioned for Theresa to stay and went to get their food.

He came back with a tray loaded with everything but the kitchen sink. She grinned as Max placed it on the wooden planks of the table, making quick time of passing out the paper plates, napkins and plastic utensils. Large paper cups filled with sweet tea accompanied the all-you-can-eat buffet overflowing the tray.

Fried shrimp, steamed oysters, fried catfish, clams, hot

spicy jambalaya, loads of French-fried potatoes and hush puppies, along with malt vinegar, lemon wedges and coleslaw were calling her name. Spreading a napkin across her jeans-clad lap, Theresa loaded her plate with a bit of everything, as Max did the same.

After the first mouthful, Theresa's eyes met Max's. A deep-fried shrimp held suspended, ready for him to bite, he waited expectantly.

"You are absolutely right. It's fabulous." She grinned and raised her glass of tea, saluting Max with it. "Good choice."

Max smiled and took a bite of the shrimp he held. "I hadn't noticed how hungry I was till I saw all this food. This place is always worth the trip."

Despite the polite conversation and his enthusiasm over the meal, she knew he'd hoped for more today.

"I'm sorry, Max." Theresa spoke softly. "I was really hoping we'd find a clue to locate Tommy."

"Yeah, me too."

For once the silence in the air wasn't filled with their usual tension, but a relatively calm, peaceful lull.

Max dangled an empty fork in front of him. "We'll probably be later getting back than we'd planned. I hope you didn't have any plans that'll be disrupted because of this trip."

"No, nothing important." She was glad the day was taking as long as it was. As much as she enjoyed her seafood, she enjoyed Max's company even more. Soon they'd be back in New Orleans and she'd be home, alone.

Holding the truck door open for her, Max glanced down

at the caller ID on his cell phone. "Brad? What's up?" He listened, his brow furrowed, before quickly walking around to his side of the truck and climbing into the driver's seat. The crease in his brow deepened.

Flipping his phone shut, he cranked the engine and turned to face her.

"We may be even later getting home. Brad says the guy who bought Tommy's Suzuki wants to make a deal. We need to head back. Now. His lawyer agreed to his client working with a police sketch artist, to give a description of the person who sold the bike to him."

"That's great, right? It's the first break you've gotten in this case." Theresa leaned over and squeezed his arm. "What are you waiting for? Let's go."

Max and Theresa made it back to the police station in record time. Within minutes they were with Brad in the interrogation room. There were already several other people there whom Brad identified as the suspect, his lawyer and the police artist.

Brad spoke quietly to Max. "You can be present while the artist does her work, but you won't be allowed to ask any questions. Understand?" Max wasn't happy about it, but he needed to get that picture. This was the closest they had come to a real lead. "Understood."

His back against the wall, he listened as the alleged suspect gave a quick description of the man from whom he had bought Tommy's Suzuki.

"An older guy, probably in his fifties. Naw, I don't know if it was early or late fifties, I'm not a good judge of anybody's age. The old guy just wanted the bike gone. His kid had died and he needed the money that the bike would bring." The suspect laughed aloud. "Guy didn't even haggle about the price I gave him. I got the thing dirt cheap."

Seated beside the sketch artist, the suspect continually peered over her shoulder to get a closer look at the picture coming to life under her fingertips. He corrected the shape of the nose here, the fullness of the mouth there, over and over making subtle changes.

The suspect's lawyer murmured unintelligibly in his client's ear then sauntered over to address Brad. "My client has cooperated with everything that's been asked of him. We've fulfilled our part of the bargain with the District Attorney's office. We're done here."

The acne-faced, stringy-haired, grease-encrusted suspect was led to the door by an officer who didn't look old enough to drink, never mind keep a creep like that in line. Max leaned over to Brad and whispered, "You sure I can't get a couple of minutes alone with him?"

Brad shook his head at Max and accepted the sketch the pretty police artist handed him. "Thanks, Annie. You're the best."

Max resisted the urge to roll his eyes. His godson's life was at stake and Brad was trying to make time with the blonde sketch artist. *Great.* Annie handed the picture to Brad, with a few flirtatious comments. She smiled briefly at Theresa and Max as she exited the interrogation room.

Brad handed the sketch over to Max. "Recognize him?"

He stared intently at the drawing, his eyes taking in every detail, each nuance, searching for a spark of recognition. Instead it was his worst fear. He didn't recognize the man depicted. The sketch was so basic, so generic, it could have been anybody.

All the expectations he'd hung his hopes on blew out of him like a rushing wind. He handed the picture to Theresa. Maybe he had one hope left. Even if he didn't know who the guy was, she might.

Theresa scanned the page from top to bottom then left to right. Her eyes narrowed and he could feel her concentration, sense her willing the page to speak to her. He wasn't sure which he saw first, the defeated slump of her shoulders or the shaking of her head. She handed the paper back to Brad.

"Let me get this processed. It'll just take a minute, and I'll get you a copy to take." Brad patted Max on the shoulder then hurried into the busy front portion of the police station. The murmur of voices could be heard through the open door.

"I'm sorry, Max." Theresa's regret-filled voice drew Max's attention back to her. She looked as sad as he felt. They were no closer to finding Tommy than when they started this search. The only new development had been the police finding his Suzuki. So far, even that hadn't amounted to anything.

"Yeah. Me too."

Chapter Sixteen

Tommy sat with his legs crossed at the ankles, the silver chain snaking across the concrete floor. Alone. *Damn it, where did Steven take Becca?*

A couple hours earlier Steven had shown up, bringing their lunch. Before leaving the tray with their disposable cutlery and paper plates, he leaned forward, gently cupping Becca's cheek. He spoke softly to her, so low Tommy couldn't hear what was said. He could read the stricken expression on Becca's face, though, and saw her barely contained tears. Tommy watched her give a bittersweet half smile then nod.

Now here he was, staring at a television set that wasn't even turned on, worrying about a girl he barely knew. He heard the crunch of footsteps on gravel outside and straightened.

They're back! As quickly as the thought occurred, another followed. *What if it's only Steven? What if Becca isn't with him?* Fear knotted his stomach. Clasping both hands in front of him, he waited.

The garage door opened and within seconds Becca's wheelchair propelled into the room, Steven gripping the handlebars. Becca sat head bowed, quiet. Even from where he stood, Tommy could see the track of tears down her cheeks.

"Are you okay?" Tommy's words sounded squeaky, rusty. He cleared his throat. "Did he hurt you?"

Steven shot him a hot angry stare. Becca shook her head. "Of course he didn't hurt me. My uncle would never do anything like that."

"Oh, yeah?" Tommy raised his foot, shaking the chain.

"Uncle Steven?" Becca looked back at the man.

"Not now, honey. We'll talk about it later."

"Gee, Uncle Steven," Tommy mocked. "Later—can you fill me in on everything, too? Like, maybe, why the *hell* you kidnapped me?" Becca cringed, flinching as though struck. Tommy hated that he'd upset her but he'd be dammed if he'd back down from Steven any more. He needed answers.

Ignoring him, Steven knelt in front of Becca's chair. "I've got to go out for a while. Will you be okay?"

Becca nodded again, reaching for the wheels. Tommy watched her roll the wheelchair forward, maneuvering into the cramped bathroom, closing the door behind her with a click. His insensitivity cost him.

Steven wrapped one hand around Tommy's throat, raising him up on to his tiptoes. Red-faced, breathing erratic, Steven looked wild. *Crazy.* Shaking him roughly, Steven threw Tommy back into the chair he had vacated when they'd arrived.

"You listen to me. I'm only going to say this once. Becca's had a bad day. Leave her alone." Steven ran a hand over his face, exhaling slowly. "I'll be back to check on her." He paused a moment. "Don't make me regret keeping you here, boy." He turned and left Tommy staring after him, mouth open, with one hand reaching for his abused throat. He could hear the turn of the lock outside, effectively sealing him back in his cage.

Damn, he's lost it. I've gotta get out of here—fast.

Becca rolled out of the bathroom, dressed for bed. Never looking at him she wheeled herself across the room, struggling to maneuver the chair into place, locking the brakes. Grabbing the sliding board, she worked to position it between the chair and the bed, and after struggling for a few minutes managed to get situated beneath the blankets.

Tommy walked over to her. He didn't know why, but he was compelled to make sure she was okay. "Are you sure you're alright?"

Becca glanced up. Tommy could see her eyes were red and he knew she'd been crying. Why that bothered him so much, he didn't know. But it did. He balled his fists so tightly his joints popped and he opened them, flexing the fingers.

"I'm fine. Really." Becca's gentle voice soothed the fury that rode inside him.

"Uncle Steven…he took me to visit my parents' grave." A single tear streaked down her cheek. "I didn't get to go to their funeral."

"Oh." What more could he say to a statement like that? Tommy wanted to reach out and wipe it away but didn't. "Do you want to talk about it—the accident, I mean?"

Becca hesitated before answering. "I think I'd like to, if

it's okay. I mean, I haven't had anybody to talk to since it happened. Except the shrink, of course." She gave a sarcastic laugh. "Can't forget the shrink they made me see after the accident. She was very sympathetic, assuring me everything was going to be okay."

Slapping her hand against her legs, she asked, "Does it look like everything is okay to you? I can't walk. I've lost my parents, I've lost my home. I've lost everything."

Tommy wasn't sure what to say or do. Perched on the edge of her bed, he awkwardly patted her hand.

"Well, I'm here. Got nothing better to do right now. And I'm a pretty good listener. Probably not as good as a professional shrink, but…"

Becca offered a weak smile. "When I woke up in the hospital, everybody was so happy. Apparently I was their miracle patient. Nobody expected me to get better. I was supposed to die, like my parents. Only I didn't."

"But that's good, right? You're alive."

"I'm alive…but I'll never walk again, never have the life I should have had."

The despondency in her tone worried Tommy. The last thing he wanted or needed was for her to get depressed.

"The life you should have had? Oh, you mean like the one I should have had before some crazy man offered me a ride, chained me like an animal and locked me away where no one will ever find me?" Tommy folded his arms across his chest. "Ah, poor baby. 'Look at me, I'm stuck in a wheel-chair.' Big freakin' deal. You're still *alive*. You still have the chance to do anything you want. I know it sounds mean, but *get over it!"* Becca's mouth opened in an *O* of surprise. Tommy grinned at her expression.

"Pity party over?"

Becca stared at him then nodded. "Pity party over."

"Good. Now tell me about your parents."

"They were the best. Not that they spoiled me or anything. They were just always there when I needed them. The night of the accident, we were on our way to see a show. It had been raining. I don't really remember what happened. I woke up in the hospital. Uncle Steven was there." Becca fidgeted with the edge of the blanket.

"And?"

"When I woke up, he cried."

Tommy couldn't picture Steven ever crying about anything. But then he didn't know the man well, did he?

"He came every day," she continued. "Uncle Steven would tell me all about this place." She waved her hand around. "He described all the things he was doing to fix it up, just for me. I asked every day about my folks, but nobody would tell me anything. It didn't take long before I figured out I wasn't ever going home again."

"So, before the accident did you spend a lot of time with your uncle Steven?"

"Enough, I guess. I mean, we spent birthdays and the holidays together, him and my mom and dad."

"I guess he wasn't always a twisted old freak who goes around kidnapping people?"

Becca gasped. Tommy knew his words were harsh, but it was how he felt. He'd lost track of how long he'd been cooped up in this converted garage, and he was damned tired of being here. Becca lost her family and he felt for her, but he still had his parents and he missed them. He wanted to go home.

"He's not. I don't know why he's done it, but he must have a reason."

"I've been here a long time and he still hasn't told me why. Tell me the person who did this isn't crazy." Tommy grabbed the chain, rattling the links, the clanking metallic sound loud in the quiet room. He stood and stepped away from the bed, his back to Becca. He could feel the angry tears in his eyes and struggled to keep them from falling.

"My folks are probably going nuts looking for me." At least, he hoped they were—looking for him, that is. Maybe they thought he'd run away. After they'd fought, when he didn't come home, maybe…

"He's all I've got," Becca said quietly behind him. "He can't be crazy, 'cause he's all I've got left."

"No, Becca. You've got me."

Chapter Seventeen

Max hadn't been driving very long, maybe fifteen minutes, before Theresa knew something was wrong. Not with Max, although he was still brooding about the lack of evidence.

"Something's not right." When he didn't respond to her words, she tried again. "Max." Her voice louder, her tone firmer. "Something's wrong with your truck." She could see wisps of smoke rising from beneath the hood. She pointed at the rising steam.

"Great, just great." With a muttered curse, Max angled the pickup to the side of the road, completely off the pavement, and killed the engine. He popped the hood release and stepped from the cab, walking around to the front. Billows of steam poured out with an angry hiss. The sputtering of boiling water could be heard. With her window down, Theresa could hear the gurgle and smell the rancid burning stench coming from under the hood.

Leaving the hood propped open, Max climbed back into the driver's seat and reached for the cell phone he had tossed there when they'd left the police station. Flipping it open, he quickly dialed a number, closing his eyes while it rang.

"Hey, Brad. Yeah, it's me. The water pump just blew on

my way out of town. Can you have a tow truck come get us?" He relayed their location, his fingers pinching the bridge of his nose. He ended the conversation with a quick word of thanks, and hung up.

"We're gonna have to be towed back to town. It'll probably be in the morning before somebody can take a look at it." He paused a moment, letting his words sink in. "We're going to have to spend the night."

Theresa glanced at her watch. It was after nine o'clock. She knew Max was right, no mechanic would be open now to work on his truck. They were stuck until morning. "It's okay. Not your fault." She hesitated before asking, "Can I borrow the phone? I need to get Maggie to cover the shop again tomorrow, since I won't be there."

Her mind was racing. She wasn't concerned about the truck, it would be fixed and they would be on their way back home tomorrow.

No, her thoughts were much more carnal. *Spend the night.* Remy had told her to fight for what she wanted, and this was like a God-given opportunity. She could have her chance to be with Max, if she just played her cards right.

Her call completed, she handed the telephone back to him, and sat back to contemplate just how she was going to make her move.

The truck driver gave Max and Theresa a ride back to town. Brad met them at the service station where they'd been towed, and gave them a loaner car along with directions to a quiet, clean motel.

Hungry and slightly nervous at the idea of spending the night alone with Max, Theresa was grateful for a short reprieve. The burger joint beside the motel offered a welcome delay.

Knowing the coming night could see them together, Theresa decided to broach a subject they had long avoided. Nine months earlier, their friendship and the rocky start of their budding romance had ended, destroyed by hurtful words said in anger and misunderstanding. The damage caused that night lingered unspoken between them.

Theresa knew the open wound of their failed relationship would continue to fester if they didn't confront the past, and like a cancer would eat away at whatever tenuous steps they took by working together. She decided to deal with all the old hurts first. *Treat it like a bandage,* she thought. Better to pull it off fast rather than prolong the pain.

"I need to ask you something. About what happened nine months ago." She watched him stiffen, his rigid posture the only indication he'd heard her.

"Yeah." He set his burger down and swallowed, hard. "I'm sorry about what happened. Really. I need to apologize. I should have apologized the next day—hell, I should have apologized when it happened, but… I guess I was ashamed." His gaze met hers, his eyes hot. She knew he was remembering the night in question.

"It was my fault as much as yours. I encouraged you. You weren't ready to hear how I felt about you, how much I cared. If anybody's to blame, it's me."

"Don't try to pull that with me, Theresa. I'm fully aware of where the blame lies. Things went way too far, too fast that night. I wasn't looking for a commitment. I took advantage of your feelings for me." He paused, confirming what she always suspected. He felt guilty about what they'd almost done, for his actions, but more for what was said afterward.

"I wanted you, Max. I invited you in, if you remember. You didn't know what had happened to me." Pausing briefly, she continued in a rush of words. "I told you I loved you." Heat rushed into her cheeks as she thought back at how bluntly she'd spoken that night. She'd been rash and foolish. She had loved him so much, still did, but she knew he hadn't been ready to hear those words.

"I'm the one who pushed things. We'd only gone out a couple of times. Up till then, we were friends." She reached across the worn restaurant table and grasped his hand firmly. "I miss that friendship. I never realized how important it was to me, until it was gone."

"That's the point," Max insisted. "I'm the one who walked away. I'm the one who made you feel like a whore. You didn't deserve that."

"You flat out told me you thought I was some kind of cock-tease, who'd led you on to the breaking point." She looked him square in the eye, deciding now wasn't the time to pull any punches. "You're right. I didn't deserve the things you said.

"You're the only man I've ever wanted sexually. The man I had loved for years." The one man whose touch sent her pulse racing. "You had me turned inside-out that night. I wouldn't have said no to you. I *couldn't*."

Max winced. He had treated her like a child. It had been a defense mechanism against how much his feelings for her changed over the years. When he came home the summer she turned eighteen, the promise of her beauty was finally less a promise and more fact. He'd fought his attraction, dating wildly to keep away from her. She'd been too young.

Living in Shreveport helped, distance making it easier to stay away from her. At least physically. The span of miles hadn't kept him from thinking about her. When he moved back to New Orleans, she'd been more beautiful than he ever dreamed. Her face no longer that of a young girl but of a sensual, desirable woman. He'd fought an inner battle but gave in to temptation and asked her out. Max never intended for it to be anything serious, just a few dates to get her out of his system. Only it didn't work out that way. The more he was around her, the more he learned about her, the more he wanted to be with her. A year ago, with his career in shambles and his life changing on a daily basis, the thought of something so permanent sent him running scared. Regret ate at him for what he'd so foolishly thrown away.

Looking at Theresa sitting across from him, he saw a stunning woman. Her long blond hair fell past her shoulders in a shiny curtain down her back, sleek and luxurious. Her green eyes, surrounded by full lashes a darker shade than her hair, shone with an inner glow, lit by her wit and intelligence. Max wanted her so badly, it felt as if the world would stop turning if he couldn't have her. He only needed to think about Theresa and he was as hard as a pike. When he was in the same room with her, his hands itched to touch her. To caress her breasts, to run his fingers over her nipples, bring them to peaking arousal. He mentally shook his head, focusing on the conversation at hand.

"I should never have said what I did. I was lashing out, frustrated and horny." Surreptitiously Max glanced around the fast-food restaurant, making sure they weren't being overheard. "The few dates we had, the kisses at the end of each, they weren't enough. I wanted more, much more than you'd have been willing to give."

"You're wrong. You could have owned every part of me. Instead you flung me aside like yesterday's garbage." Theresa's hands clutched the paper napkin she held, shredding it to jagged pieces as she spoke, her jerky movement revealing the suppressed anger behind her words. Max flinched, the harsh truth burning like acid.

"I know. It's been killing me to be near you, working this case, seeing you and not being able to get past what I said. What I threw away."

"You said I sent out mixed messages about what I wanted. That I was blowing hot and cold, keeping you and Remy both on the line while I made up my mind. You were wrong, Max. My choice was made years ago. *I chose you.*"

Max reached across the table, grabbing Theresa's hand. Silently she yanked it free, pushing to her feet. Snatching up her purse, she paused. "You coming?"

Before he could react, she was gone. He watched her sashay across the street, her hips moving sensually in those oh-so-tight jeans as she walked the short distance to their motel.

Unsure how to proceed, Max wanted to make things right with Theresa, maybe even try to start over. He cared deeply about her, and wanted to see if they could make a fresh start. He just wasn't sure how.

He joined her in front of the motel manager's office. It was Theresa who broke the awkward, strained silence. "If you truly thought I sent mixed signals all those months ago, I'm sorry. I'll try to be concise here, so there's no misunderstanding." Her steady gaze met the question in his eyes.

"I'd prefer it if you only got one room tonight. Is that clear enough?"

Chapter Eighteen

Max walked into the dimly lit interior of the motel's office, his mind reeling. Had Theresa actually said what he thought? The erection straining at the placket of his jeans was uncomfortable, anxious to spring free. He took a deep breath and requested *one* room.

Without breaking stride, he grabbed Theresa's hand and half-pulled, half-dragged her to their room. He inserted the key, his hand shaking so badly it was a Herculean task to fit the tiny piece of metal into the lock. Once it unlocked, he wrenched the key free and flung the door wide.

He gave Theresa a gentle push and followed close behind, closing and locking the door.

Grabbing her shoulders, he spun her and pressed her back against the door. He leaned in, his tall frame resting against hers. Hips met hips. He pressed close, letting her feel his straining arousal. He felt the brush of her breasts and groaned, eyes closing to savor the sensation. He had wanted for so long to hold her like this, to feel her lush supple curves and know she wanted him just as much.

He heard the catch of her breath at the contact, felt her nipples harden until they were hard pebbles pressed against his chest. Her arms went around him, hugging herself closer.

He slid one long leg between hers, his thigh brushing against her cloth-covered mound. Her passionate whimpers inflamed him. A desperate need drove him.

He bent and nuzzled his face against her neck, while he continued rubbing his thigh at the juncture of her legs. His lips caressed her nape, sweeping across one side of her exposed flesh. His teeth caught her earlobe to nip gently then lave away the hurt.

Max glanced down at the rise and fall of her breasts, her breath coming in short panting bursts. He hesitated. He had to be sure.

He stepped back, freeing her from the close press of his body against hers. He studied her face, looked for any hint of panic, any telltale sign of fear.

"Are you sure, baby? You want this?" He paused. "Me?" *Please, please be sure.*

"I love the feel of your arms around me. Your kisses drive me insane." Her hand went to the buttons on his shirt. She eased one open, then a second. Her eyes lifted to his, and he read the need there, her own desperation.

"I want you more than I've ever wanted anybody." Theresa's response was a husky whisper, her tone a blend of anxiety and a plea. "But, I'm not sure if I can do this." He stiffened slightly, waiting for her to continue.

"I haven't been able to give myself fully to anyone since the assault. I'm okay at the beginning. I enjoy what's happening. Then fear takes over, and it's like the rape all over again."

Her eyes pleaded with him, desire shining in their

depths. "I want to try with you. More than my next breath, I want to make love with you. Please, Max, please don't stop."

Max groaned as her fingers finished unbuttoning the front of his shirt. He realized she'd been working them while she talked, oblivious until he felt her hands smooth the fabric aside. He felt it slide over his shoulders and down his arms. A quick tug and it pooled on the floor at his feet, while her hands reached around front for his belt buckle.

"You've never been with any man…since that night, Theresa?" The thought caused his groin to tighten. All he could think about was sliding inside her, feeling her snug warmth surround him, encasing him in ecstasy.

She shook her head, her long hair flowing around her shoulders, partly concealing her face. She blushed, a faint pink spreading from her neck and into her cheeks. He didn't want her embarrassed; he wanted her hot. Just as hot for him as he was for her. He knew she wasn't there yet, but he hoped it wouldn't take long to get her as out of control as he felt. *Control. Maybe that's the key.* The idea took root in Max's head. He blurted it out before thinking it through.

"What if I let you have all the control? You set the pace. We can stop whenever you say the word. Hell, you can be on top, that way you can even determine how deep I go inside you." Her eyes widened, followed immediately by a beautiful, wicked smile. He knew she was thinking about taking charge of their lovemaking.

"You'd do that for me? Let me take things at my speed, my way? I didn't think guys would do that."

He grinned. "Well, honey, I'm not just any guy." His

hand rose to caress the side of her face. "I care a great deal about you. I always have. Plus, I don't want to screw this up. You deserve to love and be loved. Let me show you how it can be."

Theresa's hands returned to the belt buckle and un-hitched it, sliding the leather free from his jeans. Tossing it onto the bed, her hands unhooked the button at his waist, and slid the zipper down with gentle care, caressing the growing bulge behind it.

Max hooked his thumbs into the waistband, lowering the jeans and his boxers to the floor together, and stepped free of them.

It took all his will to stand steady and unmoving while Theresa took in the full view of his erection. It stood out firm and proud from his groin, evidence of his desire. *For her.* She remained frozen, staring, and he hoped he hadn't gotten it wrong, that the fears were more than she knew how to handle. He had to keep the situation light. No matter how badly he wanted to dive in to the hilt, this had to go slow and easy. He didn't want her to panic or become afraid, so he tried to lighten the mood.

"I think somebody in this room has too many clothes on, and it's not me." Max hoped his grin set her at ease, helped her relax.

"You're so beautiful, Max." Her voice was filled with awe as she reached out to touch him. Her fingers boldly wrapped around his shaft, her grasp firm and sure. He jerked, craving more. He hoped he didn't embarrass himself by coming in her hand, her touch felt so exquisite. "Theresa…"

"On the bed," she said, her voice firm, purposeful. He gloried in the fact her decision was made. *She's mine.* She was going to make love to him.

He bounded to the middle of the bed and lay on his back. She picked up his belt, flexed the leather, making a cracking sound as the two sides smacked together. She smiled wickedly.

"My turn."

Theresa tossed the belt across the foot of the bed and reached for the first button of her sweater. Her eyes never left his. She undid first one button, then two, followed slowly and tantalizing by the third. She continued her slow striptease until all buttons were finally open, revealing the lacy camisole underneath.

Peeling back the blue cardigan with a graceful shrug, she slid first one shoulder free, then the other. Beneath it, the silky top was delicate and feminine. Its lacy trim framed the lush bounty of her breasts. With a deliberate wiggle, she raised the hem, exposing her stomach.

Theresa saw Max swallow. A smile touched the corner of her lips before she continued. In one continuous motion, she pulled the cami up and over her head. Her breasts were finally freed. Instead of reaching up to cover them, she thrust them forward, a silent invitation for him to look his fill.

Max reached out one hand, but she stepped back. "Uh, uh. No touching or I'll have to tie you up." He laughed and lay back. Theresa hoped he was enjoying the show.

Her hands went to the top button of her jeans. Slowly she pushed one button free, only to reveal another.

Bending forward, her long hair obscuring her view of Max, she slid the jeans down her hips, past her thighs to the floor, gracefully stepping out of them, now clad only in a pair of bikini briefs. They were blue and lacy, a match for the discarded camisole. Deliberately torturing Max, she picked up the pile of clothing, both his and hers, and folded each piece carefully before laying them over the back of a chair. The anticipation was killing her, too. Theresa wanted to take things slowly, savor every sensation but a moment of doubt plagued her. Could she do this? Finish what she'd started? Always, in the past, she'd frozen the moment things started turning serious. She never even got this far with anybody else. *But then,* she thought, *they weren't Max.*

She turned around to face him, tucking her thumbs in the elastic of her panties. "Should I leave these on or take them off?" Her breasts stood out firm and full, the pink nipples puckered, aroused.

"Oh, definitely take them off."

The blue lace panties slid down her hips, one slow tantalizing inch at a time. Her fingers stopped abruptly. She bit her lower lip, eyes downcast.

"What's wrong, honey?"

"Nothing. I just thought I should tell you. In case you're worried. That…I mean…I'm on the pill. Just so you know."

"God's truth, sweetheart, I want you so much, I never gave it a thought. There's a condom in the back pocket of those jeans."

Max sat up, scooted across the bed and perched on the edge, patting the space beside him. Putting his arm around her bare shoulders, he pulled her close against his side, wrapping her in his warm embrace.

"I'm glad one of us is thinking clearly, and it's certainly not me." Theresa couldn't hold back her laugh. Running an index finger down her nose, Max grinned at her.

"As important as this talk has been, we're killing the mood here, sweetheart. Let's see if we can remember where we left off."

Theresa stood and turned to face Max. "Oh, I remember." She pointed to the bed. "Back in the middle for you, big boy." She watched as Max pushed himself back to the center, rumpling the sheets as he went.

Crawling up beside him, she tentatively reached out a hand and slowly slid it through the curling hair of his chest. She followed the pattern from one nipple to the other, then began to slowly inch her way downward.

Her fingers grazed the skin of his muscled stomach, and he inhaled sharply. She looked up into his eyes. "Am I doing something wrong?"

"You're doing everything right," Max replied, his voice trailing into a groan as her mouth covered his nipple, taking the hardened bud inside. She laved it with her tongue, gently sucking. His back arched off the mattress.

"Do you like that?" She gently blew on the tip before moving to the opposite one.

"Oh, yes," he hissed, his voice catching as she sucked the other nipple. His hands reached up, cupping her breasts.

"No, no. None of that." Theresa stared down at Max, scraping a nail across the distended nubbin. "Don't make me go for that belt."

Her gaze looked around the top of the bed, edging up to the headboard. "See if you can slide your hands under the bottom edge of the headboard, and hold on to it." She watched his hands snake toward the top of the mattress to grasp the bottom of the wood.

"You said we could do this my way, at my speed, so right now, you can't touch." Theresa swung herself up and over him, straddling his upper thighs, yet just out of distance of his erection. She still had her panties on, and she felt the moisture soaking them. Max grinned and she knew he could feel the dampness of her arousal.

His grin quickly turned to another groan, his face twisted into a grimace of pain and pleasure as her fingers teasingly walked down his abdomen, following the light shadowing of dark hair. His body tensed as if in anticipation, waiting for her touch where he wanted it most.

Her fingers gently slid along his engorged length, wrapping themselves firmly around the base, squeezing. She moved her hand forward slowly along the length of the shaft, from base to tip, then back again. "Holy mother," he growled.

Her fingertip caressed the bulbous head, catching the drop of moisture that seeped out.

"Gently, sweetheart." His voice came out in a ragged whimper as her hand moved to cup him, kneading and caressing, thrilled that she could fill him with such pleasure.

This was so much more than Theresa ever expected to feel. Always before, memories of pain and humiliation kept her from wanting to even try to have sex again. But with Max, it wasn't just sex, not for her. Her love for Max threatened to engulf her, driving her on. She wanted Max to understand—even if she never said the words again—to feel her love through her touch and know her heart was forever his.

Max's eyes flew open when Theresa's hands left his body. She lifted herself up, off his legs. He stifled a groan, wanting to cry out in need. He prayed she wasn't backing out now, not at this point. A quiver of panic ran through him at the thought. He wouldn't force anything, would never make her do something she didn't want. Panic turned to joy when she stripped off the blue lace panties. His hands gripped the rough edge of the headboard more firmly. He longed to touch her, to bring her the same exquisite pleasure she was bringing him.

Back arched, her eyes glowing brightly, she rose over him again. He could smell her arousal, feel her heat as she slid slowly down, so close, so very close to where he wanted her.

She bent forward, her hair spreading out around them both, as she leaned in to trail kisses across his chest and down to his navel. Her tongue circled, lapping, blazing fire down his groin.

"Babe, please, you're killing me."

Her head raised up just enough to see his face, tilted so

she could still fire kisses across his groin, lower and lower, tantalizing him. His engorged shaft strained upward, thicker and higher, a sweet ache.

She finally drew up straight, edging her knees farther up on the mattress, until her hot moist core was centered over his straining erection. Grasping it with her hands, she began slowly sliding down his length. He heard her breath catch as the head entered her, stretching her tender flesh as it parted. She was wet, juices flowing, ready to take him. His hands strained against the headboard, fingers clawed, and held on tight. He fought taking her hips, pushing her all the way down.

She seated herself fully, the look of awe on her face thrilling him. *Thank God.* Max flexed slightly, felt her muscles tighten around him. Beads of sweat dripped down his forehead, as he fought to keep from pumping into her. She looked at him, a question in her eyes.

"Ride me, babe. Raise up slightly, then slide down again. Find a rhythm. You'll know it."

His back arched, his body straining up to meet hers. She lifted herself up only to slide back down, muscles clenching, gripping him in a satin vise. Over and over she moved, finding her rhythm. Her body drenched with sweat, breasts glistening in the light from the bedside lamp. She closed her eyes, her face beautiful in her passion.

He could feel her body tense. Knew it would only be moments before she found her release.

"Come for me, baby. Let it go. That's it." He increased the movements of his hips, bucking wildly, driving into her, flesh meeting flesh. She raised a fist to her mouth, muffling her screams as she came. One, two, three strokes more and he joined her, calling out her name.

Slowly Theresa slid off to lie beside him. One hand curled on his chest, she leaned forward to brush a kiss across his lips.

"That was incredible."

Releasing his death grip on the headboard, Max pulled her close against his side. Smoothing the hair from around the sides of her face, he tucked it behind her ear, looking her in the eyes. Bending forward, he brushed a soft, wet kiss across her passion-swollen lips.

A smile flitted across his mouth as he whispered, "Now it's my turn."

Chapter Nineteen

Theresa smiled almost the entire drive back to New Orleans the next afternoon. Max made love to her all night long, like a starving man feasting upon his last meal. After the first time, when he had relinquished control to her, most of her fears were alleviated.

It took the edge of urgency off Max, too. The second time they made love had been slow and sweet, with such tenderness it brought tears to her eyes just remembering.

They showered, bathing each other, trading kisses and caresses and washing each other's bodies. Afterward they'd fallen asleep in each other's arms.

Just after dawn, Max awakened her with kisses, and brought her to an orgasm that exploded through her, rocking her body with wave after wave of pleasure.

They stayed in the motel room much later than they'd planned, waiting for the service station to call. Now they were back in the repaired truck, heading for New Orleans.

Theresa had something to tell Max, but with everything that had happened in the last twenty-four hours she'd forgotten.

"Max, before you picked me up yesterday, I was focusing on Tommy. Remy came by for coffee, and I forgot to tell you."

"What was it?"

"It's not much really. I saw gray walls. From the shape and texture, they looked like cinderblocks, the kind used in construction. The floor was gray, too, but a shinier, smoother texture. It was almost like what I'd picture a basement to look like, but we don't have basements in Louisiana."

Max's eyes narrowed in concentration, his hands tightening on the steering wheel, his focus never leaving the highway. "No we don't, do we? And cinderblocks are used all throughout the South in construction, not just Louisiana." He reached across and squeezed her hand. "I know you're trying, hon. We'll find him."

Unbuckling her seatbelt, Theresa slid across the bench seat to lean her head against Max's shoulder.

"I just feel so useless. I blocked my psychic abilities for so long, hated them. Maybe if I hadn't, they'd be stronger and I could find him."

"It's not your fault. You're not the sick freak who took a helpless kid." He angled his head around to brush a kiss across her forehead.

"We've still got a way to go yet, why don't you try to get some sleep?"

Closing her eyes, she relaxed and after a few minutes let sleep overtake her.

Theresa knew she was dreaming. The sights, sounds and

smells were all two-dimensional, muddied yet somehow familiar. She sat at the scarf-covered table in her store. It was closed. Only a single beam of light shone from the kitchen behind her shop. During working hours she always kept that door shut, but it was cracked open now. Across from her a young man paced, wringing his hands.

Cut in the style popular with teenagers—very short on the sides, long on the top—his hair hung straight down and kept flopping into his eyes. He reached up to brush it back, when she noticed bloody scratches on his hands and his ragged, broken nails. His faded navy blue T-shirt was ripped, the collar torn, hanging off one shoulder.

"You've got to help them." Desperation rang with each word. Again he wrung his hands together, anxious. His gaze flitted around the room, looking at all the things scattered throughout the shop, never meeting her eyes. "He's gonna hurt them."

"Them? Who are you talking about?"

"Them. Tommy Saunders and the girl."

"Tommy's missing. We're looking for him."

Level with hers, his eyes burned with a feverish gleam. "Try harder. If you don't get him soon, he's gonna kill them. Just like he killed me."

The boy turned around and walked a few steps away from the table. That's when she saw it. Blood. Thick and dark, matted across the back of his head, a massive ugly wound, clear evidence of a trauma.

There wasn't a doubt in her mind. He was dead. She'd never talked to a dead person in her vision dreams before.

And yet, she felt calm, detached. Who was this ghost?

"You keep saying them. This person who has Tommy, he has somebody else, too? Who is he? How do we find him?"

The ghost or spirit—whatever this apparition was— nodded his head.

"He has Tommy and a girl. You've got to find them, before it's too late. Help them—so you can help me, too."

Just like that he was gone, leaving her alone in the shop. She needed to wake up and tell Max they had to hurry. She couldn't let Tommy die, too. If this madman had already killed once, time was running out.

For the last few minutes Theresa had been moaning in her sleep, jerking restlessly. Max debated whether he should pull over and wake her up. They hadn't gotten much sleep the night before. He couldn't hold back a smile at the reason why. He'd go without sleep again, if he could spend another night like the previous one.

Abruptly Theresa sat upright, flinging herself forward. He barely had time to reach his right arm in front of her and brace her body to keep her from smacking head-first into the dashboard of the truck. Her breathing was rapid, her eyes glassy.

Easing on the brake, he pulled onto the paved roadside, as traffic continued speeding by. He slammed the gearshift into park before turning to face her.

"Honey, what's wrong?"

"Tommy's in danger." She blew wisps of hair out of her face, where it had been flung with her forward momentum. "I had a dream. A boy warned me that a crazy man has him and a young girl, and their time is running out." She pressed her lips together, and clenched and loosened her fingers before facing Max again.

"He said this person is going to hurt them, maybe even kill them. He said the man had killed him. He was dead, Max. The back of his head was covered in blood. Lots of blood. I've had vision dreams before, not for a long time, but this was the most real, the most intense."

Had she been anyone else Max would have offered her a drink and called a shrink. But this was Theresa. "Vision dreams? What are those?"

"It's what I call them. Sometimes when I touch something, I get a sense about it, either about who owned it, what it's been used for. Like Tommy's cell phone. But these dreams are something else. Sometimes when I have a dream, it will be about something that's already happened." A lone tear caressed a solitary path down her pale cheek.

"Sometimes, though they're rare, my dreams are about things that are going to occur." Clenching her fisted hands in her lap, Theresa murmured, "I don't know if the boy's dead yet or not, but if we don't figure out a way to find him, he'll die. And so will Tommy."

Chapter Twenty

I t was a glorious day for mid-November. The sunshine highlighted all the brilliant fall colors. Louisiana couldn't boast the magnificent foliage of other states, but today its majestic glory was in full sway. Bright reds, yellows, golds and bronzes shone on the treetops, as leaf after leaf floated effortlessly to the grassy carpet below.

Steven stood at the huge bay window in his living room and watched the leaves slowly spiral down, catch the sporadic breezes and spin merrily before stopping on his lawn. His yard was perfectly manicured, a year-round advertisement and testament to his landscaping skills.

Sadness filled him. This would be the last autumn he would see. The last time he'd watch the changes nature wrought. He'd miss the brisk mornings, gradually warming up throughout the daytime hours, sunshine permeating the sky, peeking through the clouds, only to have the temperature cool in the evenings. This was his favorite time of year. Even though it meant a drop in his landscaping business, the ever-changing fall never depressed him.

He did mind that this would be the last one, though. He wasn't ready. There was still too much unfinished.

Tommy and Becca weren't cooperating with his plan. If

Tommy weren't chained, if Becca wasn't virtually a prisoner herself without her chair, they'd never even speak.

He'd have to do something to fix that. *What could draw them together?* They needed a common goal, a target to strive for. Something other than their freedom. That would come soon enough, sooner than either of them realized. Until then, he had to come up with something to bridge the gap, make the bond between them grow and solidify.

He needed Tommy to care. That was his only hope now. Nothing else mattered.

Jacob Freeman slammed on the brakes of the ten-speed bike and dropped his feet to the ground, glancing at the house. He didn't know Steven Black. Just that he was a professional handyman and landscaper around New Orleans. He'd done some checking, and the man had a good reputation.

Normally, he wouldn't be caught dead talking to somebody like him, but he'd run out of options. He needed a part-time job and hadn't been able to find anything yet. Even with the holidays approaching, almost all the part-time positions had already been filled. He was desperate. With Christmas just around the corner, he needed money and fast.

Except for the fast-food joints, he applied everywhere. Flipping burgers was a last resort. They paid nothing—minimum wage—and had crappy hours. He needed enough money to be able to buy gifts, and get his ride fixed.

His car was an old junker and he loved it, except the hunk of junk kept needing one repair after another. Most of his savings paid the insurance and bought gas. Now it was broken down again. Having to go everywhere on this stupid bike was the pits.

Money was the key. It held all the answers, and Mr. Steven Black of Black's Back to Basics just might be the answer to his prayers.

Earlier he'd stopped by the hardware store, hoping to get a job stocking shelves, working in the garden department or even putting up the holiday displays. They were full up on part-time people, but one of the clerks had told him about this guy who had two roofing jobs lined up. He'd come in and ordered a ton of supplies. Maybe he could use some part-time help.

Jacob leaned his bike up against the side of a decorative concrete pillar flanking the entrance of the driveway. His nerves beginning to fray, he straightened his clothes, smoothed down his shirt and pulled the bottoms of his pants out from his socks where he'd tucked them before getting on the bike. He'd learned the hard way they'd get caught in the chain if he didn't.

Running a hand over his hair to make sure it wasn't standing straight up, he walked to the front door. Inhaling a deep breath then exhaling slowly, he gave a brisk knock. After a minute or two, he knocked again. No answer.

Determined, he stepped off the porch to glance through the large bay window. The curtains were cracked enough he could see inside. Nothing. *Maybe he's not home.*

Scanning the yard and debating his next move, he spotted the white pickup truck parked behind a white van. He hadn't noticed them before, but he hadn't been paying much attention, more concerned with making a good first impression.

Both vehicles were lined up with military precision on the rocky pathway next to the house. The hood of the truck still felt warm. Somebody was there.

Thinking he heard a voice, he walked toward the back of the house slowly, not wanting to get into any trouble. No, make that *voices*. He grinned. *Yes. Things are looking up.*

His stride brisk and purposeful, he followed the rocky pathway. Start as you mean to go on, his father always said. Go after what you want. He rounded the corner, pulling up short at the raised voices, steadily increasing in volume. He could feel the anger.

A building sat back about fifty feet behind the house, completely hidden from the street. It looked like an enclosed garage. No windows and only one door. Through the open doorway, angry raised voices were coming from inside.

"This is so not a good idea," he whispered, edging closer anyway. "Excuse me? Mr. Black?"

A large man barreled through the open doorway, eyes blazing, fists clenched, only to pull up short. Jacob felt the staccato rhythm of his heart racing, pounding in his throat. *Shit.* The saliva in his mouth dried, his hands trembled. Sweat broke out along his forehead.

The man braced his fisted hands on his hips. He looked like the Jolly Green Giant on steroids and mad as hell. Jacob's gaze slid past him, widening in shock. There were two other people in that garage. He recognized one of them.

Tommy Saunders. He barely knew Tommy, only enough to say hello as they passed in the halls at school. He also knew Tommy's parents had reward posters up all over town, frantically searching for him. Yet here he was, a short distance from his parents' home. *What the hell?*

Tommy's hands waved frantically, his voice called out with desperation. "Run, man. Call the cops, get help!" Tommy ran toward the door, stumbled and crashed to the floor, falling hard. *Holy hell!* A steel chain wrapped tightly around Tommy's legs, keeping him from reaching the open door.

"Shut up, you idiot!" the man shouted at Tommy as he advanced toward Jacob, each step crunching loudly on the gravel. Jacob ran. Legs pumping, arms swinging, he sped over the rocks, crying out as he bumped his hip against the bumper of the pickup truck. Pain shot through him and he stumbled, careening out of control before righting himself. Catching his balance, he continued running, yelling for help at the top of his lungs.

Strong arms grabbed him from behind, propelling him face-first onto the ground. Hard. All the air in his lungs rushed out in a dizzying whoosh. Clawing at the gravel, feeling his hands cut on the pointed rocks, he struggled to throw off the weight pinning him down.

One meaty hand grabbed his T-shirt by the collar while another gripped the waistband of his jeans. He was frog-marched back behind the house again, toward that open doorway.

"No, you sick bastard. Let me go." Fright made him

angry, adrenaline pumping as he struggled in the grip of the madman, fighting for his freedom. He swiveled his torso, balled up his fist and struck out, swinging backward and to the side. He felt the punch land. His assailant grunted from the blow, but his hold never lessened.

Jacob screamed louder, his voice raspy and hoarse. There was no way the neighbors would hear him, but he had to try. Couldn't stop. He yelled and fought.

Tommy and the other person, a girl, were screaming for the crazy man to let him go, but his hold just tightened. He heard the ragged sound of ripping material as his T-shirt rent. He pulled forward and kicked out, catching his assailant's kneecap. It worked. With a startled cry, his grip lessened slightly, and Jacob broke free.

Without hesitating, he sprinted around the corner of the house, racing for the driveway. Why hadn't he clipped his cell phone to his waist, like he always did? He'd put it in his backpack, and left it on the bike where it was useless…unless he could get to it.

He'd barely taken more than a few steps when a powerful force again hit him from behind.

"No," he wailed. "Lemme go. You can't do this, you sick pervert. Let me go." Jacob was yanked to his feet, a large muscular forearm wrapped around his neck. A solid threat to cut off his air supply if he kept struggling. He held himself rigid then dropped like a dead weight, hoping to slip out of this maniac's hands.

It almost worked, too. With the shift in his weight, he swept one leg behind, knocking the other man's legs out from under him. They tumbled to the ground in an awkward tangle of limbs. Both struggled to gain superiority. Jacob continued yelling, his voice faint, knowing he might never get another chance.

A solid uppercut landed on his jaw, throwing him backward. Excruciating pain pierced him. The other man was on him again before he'd even processed he'd been hit.

"Shut up! Shut up! Shut up!" the man wailed, screeching higher and higher. Waves of pain rolled through Jacob. With each "shut up," Jacob's head was lifted then smashed back down against the rough surface of the drive. He finally stopped screaming, stopped making any sounds, just felt the pain, sharp and unrelenting, a continuous roiling nausea as his head connected with the ground.

The edge of blackness crept ever closer on the outer edges of his vision. *Lord, no. I don't want to die.*

He stared into the brown-eyed intense look of a man driven to the brink of madness, recognizing the instant sanity returned and the man realized what he'd done.

It was the last thing Jacob ever saw.

Becca's screams echoed through the room, only partially muffled by the cinderblock walls. Tommy reached over and pried her fingers free from the armrests of her wheelchair. Her short blunt nails had left gouge marks.

He squatted in front of her, patting her hand clumsily. He didn't know how to comfort her. What can you say when somebody sees the unthinkable? An eerie quiet settled into the room, the only sounds Becca's ragged indrawn breaths as she tried to control her tears.

Steven had killed that boy. Chased him down and beat his head into the ground, over and over, until he finally stopped crying for help.

Guilt was a bitter pill to swallow. Tommy's heart ached. He'd told the kid to run. Maybe if he hadn't…maybe. Yeah, well maybes didn't amount to much when hope was gone.

He and Becca had yelled and screamed at Steven to stop. He'd been a man possessed, his actions wild and uncontrolled. Helpless, Tommy watched, unable to render any kind of aid. Steven's screams still echoed in Tommy's ears—a high-pitched, sickeningly eerie sound—yelling at the boy to shut up.

Bright red blood stained the light gray and white rocks as the kid's head came up, only to be smashed down again. Blood and dirt matted the back of his head, soaked into his blond hair.

Steven stood and stared down at his hands, horror clearly written on his face at the sight of the blood, a brilliant crimson hue in the afternoon sunshine. A solitary heart-wrenching sob broke free before he turned toward them. From his expression it was evident; he knew they had seen everything.

Steven is a murderer. He'd brutally killed Jacob. Tommy finally remembered his name. They went to the same high school but didn't have any of the same classes, which was why he hadn't recognized him at first.

Jacob had called out for Steven by name. Tommy

couldn't help but wonder what he was doing there. Now he'd never know.

Steven hadn't uttered a sound. He straightened, eyes whipping around rapidly. Satisfied nobody had seen him, he'd stalked to the open door, pulling it shut with a sharp bang. Becca flinched at the sound, her sobs quieting. Tommy heard the ominous sound of the click as the lock turned.

They were alone. Steven was gone, at least temporarily. Tommy grimaced at the thought of what might happen when he came back.

He focused on Becca's face, her eyes red-rimmed from crying. He wished he could give her time to deal with what had happened, but they didn't have time.

Stooping in front of her chair, he placed his hands on the padded armrests for balance and leaned forward, using the knuckle of his index finger to raise her chin. His gaze met hers without wavering.

His voice low but firm, he said, "We don't have much time. We need to think. What the heck are we going to do when he comes back?"

Chapter Twenty-One

Max pushed the speed limits racing back to New Orleans. Theresa had been shaken by her dream, a grim vision of death. If her prophetic dream was true…he didn't want to think about it.

He dealt with realities—hard, concrete facts—not intuition or dreams. As far as he was concerned, Tommy had been in danger from the time he'd gone missing. Each day that passed with him not home, the feeling in his gut, what he used to call his cop's instincts, went further into overdrive. Chances were, if Tommy wasn't found soon, he'd never make it back. Any cop knew, the longer a child is missing, the less likely he'll be found.

Now, here was Theresa having nightmares about a dead kid. *A psychic warning or a figment of an overactive and overwhelmed mind, trying to deal?*

He dropped her off at her apartment before heading to his office. The glare of the overhead fluorescent bulb buzzed, its harsh light flooding the rented space. Max froze. His desk was overturned, papers tossed everywhere. That mountain of filing he'd spent weeks procrastinating about blanketed his office in a layer of white pages, ripped and torn. Books were pulled from shelves. Some had ripped bindings, others lay with pages open where they landed.

Careful not to touch anything, he walked farther into the room, checking for anything missing or stolen. His gray leather chair was the only piece of furniture in the room not upended. A single sheet of paper rested on the worn seat.

Reaching down he carefully lifted the paper by one corner. He flipped it over to stare at the block letters, their edges ragged and torn as if cut from old newspapers or magazines.

STOP LOOKING FOR THE BOY. YOU WON'T FIND HIM. FOR EVERYBODY'S SAKE, QUIT LOOKING OR THINGS WON'T BE SO GOOD FOR YOU OR YOUR BLONDE LADY-FRIEND.

Fingers shaking, Max unclipped his cell phone from his belt and dialed 9-1-1. Assured the police were on their way his second call was to Remy.

"Hey, bro. Need you to do something for me. No questions, okay? Get over to Theresa's place right now and keep an eye on her. No, I'll be over later, but it'll take some time, maybe a couple hours."

He knew his brother had questions, but right now he didn't have time to spell it out for him.

"Max, what the hell—"

He interrupted Remy in mid-protest. "Look, I need a pair of eyes I can trust watching her back now. She's been threatened."

"I'm on my way. I'll be there in less than five minutes."

Max's shoulders drooped. He knew he wouldn't relax until he was with Theresa, and could hold her in his arms to reassure himself she was okay.

The sound of footsteps outside his office doorway announced the police's arrival. Their professional gazes swept the scene and the destruction of his office. Max breathed a sigh when he recognized Etienne Boudreau and his partner. He'd know Etienne for years, going back to their childhood. Although he was a few years older than Etienne, Max knew the other man well. Etienne's older brothers, Jean-Luc and Ranger, were friends, had been since they were rowdy teenagers fooling around in the bayou where the Boudreau family lived.

"This was on the seat of the chair." Max handed the threatening note to Etienne, and watched as he placed it in an evidence bag. They'd run it for fingerprints as well as dust the entire office. He had a gut feeling they wouldn't find anything. Somebody wanted to make a real statement here, but he didn't think they were stupid. They wouldn't have left any evidence behind.

With this letter, though, Max had solid proof Tommy hadn't run away. He'd been kidnapped.

Theresa opened the door to find Remy on the other side. A quick look at his face and she knew something was up. Having known him for nearly half her life, she could always tell when he tried to hide something, and he was firing on all cylinders right now. Varying emotions flitted across his face, so rapid she couldn't get a handle on what he was feeling.

"Okay, what's going on?"

"Nothing. I mean—I just stopped by to see how things

went in Mississippi."

"Sure you did." She gave him a good hard look and knew he was lying through his teeth. "Hogwash. You had to work tonight. Max sent you here. Why?"

With a sheepish grin, Remy grabbed her into a hug, swinging her around in circles, once, twice, three times, holding her close.

As a distraction, it worked for all of two seconds, before Theresa pushed firmly against his chest, freed herself and stepped back. "Uh, uh, not gonna work, Slick. Why'd Max send you?"

"Don't know." Remy's lips cocked up in a wicked grin.

Theresa sent him a probing look.

"Really," he swore, "I don't know why he sent me. He said he'd explain when he got here."

"Okay. I'll wait. Since it'll be a while before he gets here, let's go upstairs."

"How do you know how long it'll take him to get here?" he asked. Theresa gave him a mysterious smile in response.

Remy smacked a hand against his forehead, making a "duh" sound.

"Right, Ms. Psychic. You know all and see all. You wanna tell me why I'm here then?"

She grinned, suppressing a laugh. Grasping his hand, she pulled him through the kitchen and up the narrow staircase to her apartment to wait for Max.

Max didn't even pause when he reached Theresa's place. He

slid open the back door and strode inside. A glance confirmed her shop was closed up tight, the lights extinguished. Upstairs, he heard the quiet murmur of voices followed by a roar of laughter. Recognizing his brother's booming tone, he took the stairs two at a time, drawing up short when he reached the top.

Theresa sat in an overstuffed chair covered with a floral pattern in sage greens, creams and peach tones, the colors soft and muted. His brother stood directly behind her. He was pulling a hairbrush through the length of her long blond hair. The strands shone, highlighted by the gleam of light projecting from a cream-colored lamp.

Max watched as one slow stroke followed the next. Theresa's eyes were closed, her full lips curved upwards at the corners. Her face glowed in the diffused light as the brush made its sensual trip down the length of her hair, guided by his brother's hand.

The ease and familiarity of his brother's grip on the brush sent a surge of jealousy racing through Max, unexpected and unwarranted, he knew. His mind told him there was no reason to be jealous of his own brother.

His heart, however, didn't follow the same logic as his brain. It ached at seeing another man's hands on his woman. The thought made him pause. *His woman.* It felt right. Even before last night, it was the truth. He'd been running from his feelings for years, hiding from the fact he was in love with Theresa.

He should have felt pole-axed by the admission, but he didn't. Instead, it felt like the most natural thing he had ever done, to let it finally come out, an accepted and acknowledged fact. He was in love with her. He wanted a chance at a future with her. In order for that to happen, though, he had to keep her safe.

"Hey, guys." Both heads turned toward him. The hairbrush stopped its momentum, a brief respite, before continuing its hypnotic journey through the length of Theresa's hair. *Damn,* he thought, *I'm jealous of a bloody hairbrush getting to touch her when I can't.*

Stomping across the short distance, he yanked the brush from his brother's hand. Remy relinquished it without a struggle, holding up both hands in surrender as he stepped back. Max knew Remy fought not to laugh, a battle he was losing, so he punched him in the shoulder. "Shut up."

Stepping around to the front of the chair, he knelt in front of Theresa and reached out his hand. He ran his fingertip along her lower lip. Her breath hitched at his gentle touch, her eyes staring into his. He leaned in, caught in her gaze, and replaced his fingertip with his lips. His kiss was a whisper of touch, a quick flick of his tongue along the seam of her lips. His tongue slid forward when her mouth opened in sweet greeting to his penetration, slick and wet.

The sound of Remy's smothered laughter kept him from deepening his kiss. He pulled back reluctantly.

"Hi, honey. You okay?" He kept his voice soft, caring.

"I'm fine," she answered. "Why wouldn't I be?"

Max raised his eyes to meet his brother's. Remy just shrugged and shook his head.

"Oh no, you don't." Theresa shook her finger under his

nose. "He hasn't told me anything. He didn't have to. I knew you'd sent him the minute he walked in the door. I want to know why."

"Me, too," Remy chimed in.

Max led Theresa over to the sofa, pulling her down next to him, close enough that he could keep his arm wrapped around her. The need to touch her, to know at this moment she was safe nearly overwhelmed him. He motioned for Remy to take the chair Theresa had vacated.

"After I dropped you here this afternoon, I went to my office. I wanted to make some copies of the sketch we picked up in Mississippi, distribute it to some of the guys on the force, give Remy a copy, and ask around a bit." His gaze met Remy's as he spoke.

"When I got to the office, it had been trashed. Somebody was looking for something. I'm not sure what but the place was torn apart. I found a note on my chair. It was from the jackass who has Tommy, warning me to stop looking."

"Son of a…" Remy's voice broke off at the look on Theresa's face.

"That's not all, though, is it?" she chided him.

"I called the cops, gave them the note and left them taking fingerprints, though I doubt they're going to find anything."

"Max, do you think I'm stupid? You'd never have sent Remy over here, without a word, for no reason. There was more to the note, wasn't there?"

Max glanced down at their entwined fingers, not wanting to give her a direct answer, but knowing it would come out inevitably. "There was a not-so-subtle threat against me...and you."

Remy exploded out of his chair, rage burning in his eyes. "He threatened you? Some scum-sucking piece of garbage threatened you?"

Theresa sat with her mouth ajar as her friend rained down obscenities on the head of the kidnapper, detailing what he was going to do to him when they caught him. She'd never heard Remy use that kind of language in all the time she'd know him. Sure, he was a cop, and that's pretty much how cops talked most of the time. She'd been around enough of them to know that. But he'd always been careful to watch his language around her.

"Yeah," Max said when Remy paused for breath. "They threatened me. That's no big deal, I can handle it. I'm more worried about Theresa."

"You don't need to worry about me. I can take care of myself," she protested.

"Nobody's saying you aren't capable of taking care of yourself. But we're talking about a criminal, a kidnapper, who has threatened you. That makes it personal."

While they argued, Remy answered his cell phone and moved to the other side of the room in search of a moment of privacy. A minute later he broke into their conversation. "Okay, I've got to go to work tonight. They're too short-handed for me to take off. After tonight, I've called in some favors with the captain, and I'm yours for as long as you need me."

"Thanks, bro." Max left Theresa's side long enough to pull his brother into a tight hug.

"I'll take tonight, and we'll work out the details in the morning."

"Not a problem." Remy nodded. "You're both too important to me for some maniac to get away with screwing around with your lives. We'll catch this bastard and he'll pay." Walking to Theresa, Remy knelt in front of her. He placed a finger under her chin and tilted her face up to his. Her mouth was set in a stubborn line, refusing to meet his eyes.

"Ter, babe, listen to Max. We know you can take care of yourself. We're not questioning that." Leaning forward, his voice barely above a whisper, he confided, "I'm more worried about him right now. This whole thing has him off-kilter. Between Tommy and you, things are spinning out of control, and that's not something he's used to. Let him take care of you tonight."

Theresa glanced up at Max for a fleeting moment then looked back at Remy. She nodded her head, gave him a quick peck on the cheek, got up and walked into her bedroom, giving the brothers few minutes alone.

"Don't push her too hard, Max. She's right, you know, she's tough. She's had to be to have lived the life she has and made it through whole."

"I know. She's not the problem. It's that sick freak who's

got Tommy out there. Nobody knew she was working with me on this except Tommy's parents and Brad. None of them would have said a word. How'd he find out about Theresa?"

"I don't know, but we'll find out. I'll be back by in the morning, and we'll work out a schedule so somebody's always with her."

Walking out of Theresa's apartment, Remy frowned. His brother was finally coming to his senses about Theresa. Looking upward at the light shining out of the window one story above, Remy made a solemn vow. Nothing and no one was going to tear his brother and Theresa apart. *God help the person who tries.*

Chapter Twenty-Two

Max sat up and groaned, rubbing the back of his neck. He'd spent a miserable night on the sofa in Theresa's living room after Remy left. She was being unreasonable. A direct threat had been made against her, and she thought she could handle it on her own. *Not a chance I'm gonna let that happen.*

He'd planned on spending another night like the one they'd shared in Mississippi, holding her and making love till the early morning hours. She had other ideas.

She'd come out of her bedroom right after Remy left, carrying a pillow and blanket. Tossing them onto the sofa, she walked back into her room and closed the door, a solid buffer between them. Max felt she was being unreasonable about the whole situation, but he wasn't going to push her. *Not yet, anyway.*

Forehead on his palms, he groaned again at the sledge-hammer pounding in his brain.

"Something wrong? Get up on the wrong side of the sofa?" At Theresa's quiet voice his head snapped up. The scent of coffee permeated the air. He sniffed, rubbing at his eyes with his knuckles, before he blindly reached in the direction of her voice. Seconds later a steaming mug of coffee filled his hand. Eyes closed, he lifted the cup and drank.

"Thanks, hon. I've got to tell you, this couch has to be one of the most uncomfortable ones I've ever slept on." He stood and stretched, joints creaking audibly, his shoulders stiff from his nocturnal contortions. He scratched a hand over his naked stomach. In deference to Theresa's modesty, he kept his boxers on, but the rest of his clothes were folded over the back of a chair.

He could feel Theresa's eyes on him, his morning erection growing even harder at the knowledge that she watched him, desire in her gaze. "Still mad at me?"

"No. I've had time to think about what you and Remy said. Maybe—and I mean just maybe—you're both right. If the person who has Tommy knows I'm working with you, he could see me as a threat. Plus, after that dream yesterday, I think this person is more dangerous than we ever thought. So, I'm willing to let you keep an eye on things. For the moment."

"Glad you see things more clearly this morning, babe. Now, come here." He sat his coffee down on the end table then spread his arms wide. Theresa stepped into them, her hands sliding around him, fingertips gliding up his back, caressing his shoulders. Her light touch sent a wave of lust straight to his groin. He'd woken up hard, thinking about her, and her touch magnified his desire, hardening his shaft to a painful stiffness.

Max dipped his head, nuzzling his nose to hers before claiming her mouth. She tasted fresh, a mixture of coffee, toothpaste and the unique taste of Theresa herself. His tongue slid forward, caressing hers. He eased back to playfully nip her lower lip, catching it between his teeth and tugging. He traced it with the tip of his tongue before invading her mouth. A groan escaped as her breasts pressed against his chest.

"I can come back in an hour, if you'd like." Remy's barely suppressed laughter had the two of them springing apart. He held up a bag in one hand, waving it hypnotically back and forth, the Café du Monde logo prominently displayed.

"Of course, if I leave, I'm taking these with me."

"Oh, no you don't." Theresa snatched it out of Remy's hand and headed for the stairs. "There better be beignets in here."

Theresa's voice trailed behind her as she headed down the stairs. "Get dressed, Max, and meet us in the kitchen. We've got plans to make."

Max raced to dress. Remy would hog all the food if he didn't hurry. His fingers were still working the buttons on his shirt when he reached the bottom step. Remy sat at the kitchen table and Theresa stood by the sink, neatly arranging the pastries onto a plate. The morning sunlight angled in through the window and caught the rose stained-glass suncatcher. Prisms of color, vivid pinks and blushes of red, sparkled onto the countertop. Max thought he'd never seen a sight more breathtaking than Theresa at that precise moment, surrounded by the sights and sounds of the morning. She took his breath away.

Although she'd acknowledged the danger of the situation, he knew he still had a fight on his hands to get her to accept any type of protection. She was a stubborn, independent woman. It was one of the many things he loved about her.

"I've taken some personal time, so I'm free for as long as you need me." Remy's voice broke the quiet of the kitchen. Max nodded, taking another sip from his coffee, his gaze darting to Theresa. She'd paused, the slightest hesitation, one hand still inside the bag as she removed the beignets. Completing the motion, she added another to the already-loaded plate before bringing it to the table. She placed the warm treat on the table and joined the two men.

"I know you guys think I need a babysitter. I don't agree, but I'm willing to compromise. To a point." Theresa wrapped both hands around her mug of steaming coffee, her rings twinkling in the morning light. "You both have lives, careers helping people. You have to keep working. I'll continue working, too. Nobody's going to bother me during the day. People are always in and out of the shop. We can work something out for the evenings, but there's no reason for your jobs to be disrupted."

"Not a chance." Max's voice was firm but filled with compassion. "Since we haven't got a clue who this person is, we can't be sure he won't waltz right into your shop during a regular workday." He stood and paced around the confines of the kitchen.

Here we go again, Theresa thought, nibbling her lip to suppress a smile. He reminded her of a large jungle cat, stalking his territory. She rolled her eyes at Remy, and he shrugged, smirking into his coffee mug.

Max stopped and stood with his arms akimbo, frowning at Remy. "What's so funny?"

"You are, bro," he quipped. "Can we keep the pacing to a minimum?"

Scowling, Max stalked back and sprawled in his abandoned chair. "Okay, fine. Help me make this hardheaded woman understand she can't be alone, even at work."

"I'm actually on your side, Max. I think she needs watching, too." Remy chimed in. "Babe, I'm not saying you can't take care of yourself. I know you can. I'm the first to say you're amazing. But this isn't a normal situation here. Until we get a better handle on this person, they're a threat." He paused a second. "I need to keep an eye on both of you."

Max snorted at that. Remy thought he needed a babysitter now? He was an ex-cop, a private investigator. He had training and he carried a weapon. Besides, they were here about Theresa, not him.

"We can work something out on hours, set up shifts. I need to get a couple hours sleep then I'm good to go." Remy stopped talking long enough to stuff his mouth full of the still-warm beignet, his gaze continually shifting between his brother and his best friend. "I heard something at the station at the end of my shift. Thought you might find it interesting. Parents came in late last night to report their son missing." He paused then added, "Another seventeen-year-old."

Max straightened, alert. "Another seventeen-year-old boy?"

"Yep. His folks apparently came in about two in the morning to report him missing. Since he hasn't been missing for twenty-four hours yet, station's doing the routine checking, but I thought you might be interested."

Reaching into his pocket, he pulled out a scrap of paper. "Brought you the information, name and address. Figured you'd want to check it out. I doubt there's any connection, but hey at this point we're grasping at straws anyway."

Max glanced at Theresa. She stared back. "Okay, fine," he conceded. "Call Maggie and see if she can watch things again. We'll go talk to—Mr. And Mrs. Freeman."

★ ★ ★

Steven knew he'd made a big mistake. He'd panicked after what had happened with the kid. He didn't understand what was happening to him. Rage consumed him, eating away at what remnants of sanity he had left. Blackness had filled his mind when the boy ran, screaming for help, yelling for the police. Steven snapped.

The police couldn't come. Not yet. Not when everything was so close to being finished. That interfering boy had almost ruined everything.

He hadn't meant to hurt him, just grab him and stop his screaming. Then lock him in with Tommy and Becca. It wouldn't have been for long.

Damn, he didn't even know the kid's name. That was

important, somehow. *You really should know the name of someone you've killed.*

But he made a big mistake going to Lamoreaux's office. Steven had wanted to see what he had on Tommy's disappearance. Did any of the evidence gathered point to him?

Instead, he had another one of his blackout spells. They were getting more frequent, and he was losing longer and longer periods of time.

When he'd come to and comprehended where he was and what he'd done to the office, he was appalled.

He left the threatening note, even cut the words and letters out of magazines and newspapers he found lying around.

He chuckled. Bet the police were going to get a kick out of the fact the note had been generated right there in that very office. They wouldn't know it had been a spur-of-the-moment idea. Let them think it had been preplanned. He'd left the used magazines behind with their gaping, cut-out holes. *Let's see what they think about that,* he thought gleefully.

Now, Steven needed a plan to dispose of the boy's body. Guilt assailed him, like vultures gnawing on a carcass, pecking at his conscience. With all he'd done recently, it surprised him that he still had a conscience. He'd become a monster. God had turned his back on him. The devil, though, would be welcoming him with open arms really soon.

Becca watched Tommy pace the length of the room, the chain draped across his arm. He carried it just about everywhere since she'd started moving around in her chair. It gave her better accessibility, and she wasn't halted when her wheels ran into the links lying across the floor.

She knew she could wheel over the chain, if she tried hard enough to put extra strength behind her pushes, but his thoughtfulness about moving it out of her path made a big difference.

He'd changed in the last day, though. Ever since her uncle had hurt that boy. She wouldn't, couldn't believe he was dead. That would make Uncle Steven a murderer, something she couldn't accept. He was a kind, gentle man, always jesting, with a good word for everybody. Though she had seen what happened, there had to be another explanation.

Tommy stopped pacing to stand in front of her, hands on his hips. The length of chain now lay on the floor, coiled like a snake ready to strike at unsuspecting prey.

"Have you come up with any way of getting us out of here?" Becca whispered her question softly, her head tilted back to look him in the eye.

Tommy squatted beside her. His pacing had done nothing except release some pent-up frustration. He was going stir crazy, needing to act yet not knowing what to do.

Steven was completely out of control, there was no denying the fact. He'd had bad moments from time to time since he'd taken Tommy, but nothing like yesterday. Killing Jacob, bashing his skull into the ground until it was a bloody pulp, put all his prior actions beyond redemption.

Tommy knew there was no reasoning with his captor now. With that single act of violence, the maniacal gleam he'd seen in Steven's eyes as he locked the door that final time, Tommy knew Steven had passed the point of no return. There would be no going home from this alive, unless he and Becca escaped. They had to come up with a plan, and fast.

"I've got nothing." The despondency filling her voice tugged at his heart.

"Look, I don't know when he's coming back, could be any minute. We have to find a way out of here now."

"It was a mistake. You saw. He didn't mean to hurt that boy."

"Mistake? Hell, no, it wasn't a mistake. He didn't just give him a little boo-boo and send him home. He *killed* him! Get it through your thick skull, right now. He may be your uncle, but he's a killer, and we're witnesses. We gotta get help, get to the police."

Tommy's harsh words made Becca flinch, and inside he winced, knowing he'd hurt her. But they needed to get out, somehow, before Steven came back.

"You're right, okay! But he's family. He's all I've got. He'll have to go to prison, won't he?" Her eyes glistened with unshed tears as she fought back sobs.

Outside noises could be heard, footsteps right beyond the door. Tommy stepped back from Becca at the click of the lock being opened. The door slowly yawned inward.

Steven strode confidently into the garage, acting as if nothing had happened. He glared at Tommy, walked forward and brushed a gentle kiss across Becca's forehead. Tommy caught her involuntary flinch and downcast gaze, her refusal to acknowledge her uncle's presence.

"I've got your tray outside, honey." He pointed at Tommy. "Step back over there, against the wall."

Once Tommy had done as ordered, Steven walked back outside, reappearing with a trolley laden with breakfast foods. Tommy's stomach growled at the tantalizing smells. Bacon, scrambled eggs, hash browns, pancakes, toast and fresh fruit in mountainous portions filled the tray. One of those plastic containers of orange juice and a bottle of maple syrup completed the picture. The amount of food was more than enough for two people, they could munch on this all day long.

"I'm not eating that." Tommy's voice filled the room, firm and cold.

Steven looked at him in surprise. Becca stared at him too, and he saw the flicker of understanding in her eyes.

"Me either," she stated.

"What's wrong with the food?" Steven asked, his voice laced with shock.

"How do we know you didn't poison it or drug it?" Tommy's voice was laced with a mix of suspicion and scorn.

"You're kidding, right? I've fed you for days now. Haven't poisoned you or drugged you."

"That was before you killed somebody right in front of

me though, wasn't it?"

Steven's expression hardened. Grabbing up one of the plastic utensils, he shoveled a forkful of the eggs into his mouth, followed by a slice of the bacon. Ripping off a piece of pancake, he drizzled some syrup on it, his eyes constantly on Tommy as he shoved that, too, into his mouth. After swallowing, he poured juice into one of the plastic cups, downing it in one quick gulp. Wiping his hand across his mouth, he asked, "There, are you satisfied?"

"No," Tommy replied. "I won't be satisfied until I'm home and you're in jail—or dead, whichever comes first."

Steven unloaded the food from the trolley, placing it on the table they used for their meals. He rolled it out the door and onto the grass beyond. Turning back, he stepped up to Becca's chair. Throughout this entire exchange, she'd refused to say another word to him.

"Honey, I know you're mad. You don't understand what's happening right now, but you will. I promise you will. Just give it some time, okay?"

"I'll understand?" Her voice dripped with sarcasm. "You promised to take care of me after the accident. Told me you'd fixed up a place where I could be by myself. I get here and you're holding somebody hostage or whatever. Then, I watch you kill somebody. I told myself over and over that you'd just hurt him, that he was going to be okay, but that's a lie, isn't it?" She slapped the arm of her chair. "He's dead. Tommy's a prisoner. I'm pretty much in my own private hell. You know what, Uncle Steven? You can just kiss my butt. I don't believe a word you say anymore."

Whipping her chair around, she started to wheel away from him, but was brought up short by Tommy's chain. Before she could even say the words, Tommy lifted it out of her path. With an angry glare over her shoulder toward her uncle, she rolled away from them both.

Through all this, Steven's eyes narrowed into slits, his mind whirling. His niece hated him right now and understandably so. But watching the interaction between Tommy and Becca, he smiled inside, knowing the bond he'd hoped for was forming, cementing them together in a camaraderie of shared experience.

He prayed it would be enough to withstand what was to come. It was his only hope.

Chapter Twenty-Three

The Freeman home was an unassuming dwelling close to the outskirts of Metairie, but still within New Orleans proper. A small white house, it showed signs of wear, peeling paint. A cracked sidewalk led to the front door. The yard was surrounded by a chain-link fence that went right up to the city sidewalk, bordered by a patch of weathered grass at the curb.

Two cars were parked at the house, one on the street and another older vehicle in the driveway inside the fence. The hood of this car was raised and a man worked diligently beneath it, changing the oil.

Max parked his truck and he and Theresa walked up to the fence, stopping at the latched gate.

"Excuse me." Max's voice broke into the silence. "Is this the Freeman residence?"

The man straightened under the hood to stare at them. "Yep. I'm Frank Freeman, can I help you?" He wiped the oil stains from his hands on a dirty orange cloth as he walked toward the gate.

"Mr. Freeman, my name's Max Lamoreaux. This is Theresa Crawford. I'm a private investigator, looking into the disappearance of a young man." Max watched as the older man's posture stiffened. He hurried on. "I understand from the police that your son didn't come home last night. I wondered if we might talk for a few minutes?"

"You working with the police, Mr. Lamoreaux?" He eyed Max up and down, gauging him. Obviously he passed inspection, because Mr. Freeman reached over and unlatched the gate. It slid open with a faint squeak.

"Used to be a cop," Max answered, sidestepping the question without actually lying. "Worked Homicide and Vice for several years before I went out on my own."

They walked up the rough sidewalk, and climbed the two steps that led to the front porch. Mr. Freeman motioned for them to have a seat on an old metal glider, big enough to hold Theresa and him if they sat close.

"My son, Jacob, didn't come home last night. Not like him to stay out without leaving word, so his ma got worried. Wouldn't rest until we went to the police. Talked with the Metairie cops, then with the New Orleans cops." He gave it the southern pronunciation "N'awlins." He pulled out the orange rag he'd used earlier and wiped at his hands again. Watching him, Max felt it was more a nervous habit rather than trying to get any actual dirt off his hands. He understood that. It gave the man something to do while he talked.

"Cops said he ain't been missing long enough to start an official-like search. Said they'd put the word out on the streets, maybe talk with some of Jacob's friends." He eyed Max again, his eyes narrowed. "That why you're here? Cops send you?"

"No, Mr. Freeman. As I said, I'm investigating the disappearance of another young man, the same age as your son. I'd like to ask you a couple of questions, if you wouldn't mind."

The screen door leading into the house opened, and a petite, middle-aged blonde woman stepped onto the porch. Her eyes were red-rimmed, as though she had been crying. Max assumed this was the mother. She looked like the type who'd call the police if her baby was missing.

"Frank, what's going on?" She looked at Max and Theresa seated on the glider. Max rose to his feet quickly. "Are you from the police department? Have you found my Jacob?" She raced forward, grasping her husband's hand in hers, her eyes never leaving Max, her expression filled with hope.

"Naw, honey, they ain't from the cops. Mr. Lamoreaux and Ms. Crawford here are private investigators." Max didn't correct him, but he heard Theresa's quickly disguised, inelegant snort rapidly turn into a cough.

"They's working on the case of a different missing kid. Mr. Lamoreaux heard from the police about Jacob being missing, and he wanted to ask us a couple of questions."

"Another missing boy?" Suspicion laced her statement. "What's this got to do with my Jacob?"

"Ma'am, we're not sure there is anything connecting the two cases at all. I just wanted to get additional information from you, if it's not too much trouble. Maybe while working the case I'm on, I might be able to get some information about your son, as well."

"Of course. I'm sorry. I'm just so worried about my boy. It's just not like him to do this, be gone overnight without telling anybody."

She gestured toward the car parked in the drive, continuing, "Told the police if he was gonna run off, he sure wouldn't leave his car here, now would he? That boy loves that car, always tinkering with it. Needs a new starter right now." She started weeping again. "I'd been saving up for weeks, I was getting it for him for Christmas." Sobbing, she leaned against her husband's chest, and his arms went around her, pulling her close.

"I'm sorry, Mrs. Freeman." From the corner of his eye, Max caught movement beyond the screened door, inside the house. He could make out a little girl, who looked to be about eight or nine years old. He noted Theresa saw her, too. Without a word he watched Theresa stand and walk over to Mrs. Freeman, and whisper something in her ear. With a nod, Mrs. Freeman pointed and whispered something back to her. *Good girl,* he thought, *she's going to go talk to the kid.*

Theresa moved quietly into the house, taking in the spotless interior. The woman kept a clean home. The furniture reflected the same care-worn appearance as the exterior, but it was spic-and-span. Following the directions she'd received outside, she walked down the hall to the bathroom, again noting that it was well cared for. They obviously loved their home and did the best they could to maintain it, making ends meet on a limited income.

Thinking she'd stayed in the bathroom just long enough to avoid looking suspicious, Theresa cracked opened the door quietly and slipped through it. From the corner of her eye, she saw a figure whip past the opening of the hall and dart around the corner.

Moving slowly so as not to frighten her, she glanced at the photos along the wall of two children, a boy and a much younger girl, both towheaded with sparkling blue eyes. They appeared so happy in those pictures, with the blissful unawareness of childhood, not a care in the world.

Keeping her eyes focused on the pictures, making inane cooing, appreciative noises, she spotted the girl's blond head peeking around the corner before whisking back out of sight.

Taking a few steps farther toward the living room, she called out, her voice barely above a whisper, "Hello. I'm Theresa. What's your name?"

For endless moments only silence greeted her. Hearing a scuffing sound, she turned and saw the girl standing in an opening that obviously led to the kitchen.

"I'm Molly. Whatcha doing here?"

"Hi, Molly. My friend Max and I came to talk to your mom and dad." Taking a step forward, she stopped when Molly stepped backward into the kitchen. She really didn't want to spook the child.

"I was looking at the pictures in the hallway. Is that you?" Molly nodded her head shyly, her lips turning up at the edges in a bashful smile.

"My goodness, you've really grown up to be a pretty young lady, haven't you? Must be those gorgeous blue eyes of yours. I always wanted blue eyes when I was growing up, but I got stuck with these old green cat eyes."

Molly took a step forward, trying to get a better look at her eyes.

"Is the boy in the pictures your brother Jacob?" she asked. Molly nodded her head, but remained silent.

"Max and I heard he didn't come home last night. That's why we came to talk to your folks. We're looking for somebody else, and we thought maybe we could look for him at the same time."

Molly looked so sad it nearly broke Theresa's heart. "I'm scared for Jacob," Molly whispered. "He promised me he'd be home before dark, and he always keeps his promises."

Theresa held open her arms, and Molly hesitated only a moment before launching herself into her embrace. Her tiny frame shook with her hiccupping sobs.

"He made me promise not to tell Momma and Papa where he was going yesterday. Did I do wrong? It was a promise, and you're always supposed to keep your promises. That's what Jacob always told me." Her voice caught, breaking into a squeak at the end.

Theresa's heartbeat sped up. Maybe this was it. She had that feeling she got when something was about to happen, that subtle psychic tingle which meant she was on the right track.

"Molly, do you know where Jacob went yesterday?" At Molly's nod, she forged ahead cautiously. She had to be very careful not to scare the girl. She was already so upset. "Can you tell me, honey? Maybe Max and I can go get him and bring him back home. And your parents would be so proud of you for helping to find him. I promise you they won't be mad that you broke a promise. Jacob won't be mad, either. Sometimes promises have to be broken, when it means helping somebody else. Please, Molly, talk to me. Where did Jacob go yesterday?"

Her lower lip quivered, but Molly met her gaze straight on. "'Cause it's getting real close to Christmas, Jacob wanted to get some money. To buy some really good presents this year. He was gonna go look for a job yesterday. After school. He wanted to get Momma and Papa something really special. He was going to buy me a new bicycle."

"Did he say where he was going to look for a job, Molly?"

"Nope. He said after school he was going to start asking places, checking at some of the stores. He said lots of places hire extra people—'cause of the Christmas shopping."

A myriad thoughts swirled through Theresa's mind. It all sounded so innocent, yet something was missing. Some vital clue, a piece to the puzzle wasn't there. It eluded her grasp, floating in the ephemeral plane. So close and yet so far.

"Molly, I think you're a very brave girl, but I need you to be really strong right now. Okay?" Molly took a deep breath and nodded her head. Reaching down, Theresa held out a hand, and Molly slid her little fingers into hers, grasping it tightly, trustingly. Together they walked to the front door, to tell the Freemans and Max just where Jacob had been the day before.

Molly's parents cried harder when she finished telling her

tale. Frank Freeman rubbed the back of his work-worn hand over his face, swiping at the tears.

"That boy, doing something like that. It's just like him, you know? Mature beyond his years, always has been. I hadn't been out to the shed in back, so I didn't notice his bicycle was gone. Darn fool kid." His voice broke, and he turned away, trying to rein in his emotions.

Max wanted to pace, but the confines of the porch left no room for it. He stuck his hands into his pockets, rolling coins around, a meager thing, but it helped. He waited until the parents had regained their composure.

"Mrs. Freeman, we'll keep an eye out for your son, ask around some. It'd help if you have a current picture we could show people." She hurried back into the house. From the corner of his eye, he watched Theresa sitting on the glider, talking softly with the girl. He was so proud of her. She'd gotten the baby sister talking as smooth as silk. Max turned toward Mr. Freeman.

"I'll check around some of the local stores, fast-food places, see if anybody remembers seeing Jacob. I'll let you know as soon as I find out anything."

"Mr. Lamoreaux, I can't afford to hire you to look for my boy. I'm strong, though, an' I can do just about any physical work you need. I'll work off any debt real quick."

"Don't worry about money, that's not important. Your son's what matters." Knowing the man's pride would be hurt at outright charity though, he added, "We'll work something out once we find Jacob."

Mrs. Freeman came bustling back out the door, a framed

photograph in her hands. Looking down at it, she touched the image before handing the photo to Max.

"Will this do? It was taken a few months ago, his school picture. We buy them every year."

"Yes, ma'am, this will do fine. I'll give you a call as soon as I have any information."

They walked down the cracked sidewalk and back out to the street where the truck was parked. Once inside, Max took the picture and looked at it closely. It was a typical high-school class photo. Jacob had shaggy blond hair, cut shorter on the sides and left longer on top, and big blue eyes. He smiled cheerfully out from the photo, full of life, a mischievous gleam shining through his expression.

Handing the photo over to Theresa, he stuck the key in the ignition and turned on the engine. At Theresa's sudden indrawn breath he turned to face her.

"Oh, God, no." He watched the blood drain from her face, leaving her frighteningly pale.

"I knew when I saw the pictures in the house…but he looked much younger in those. He's the boy from my dream. The one who told me we had to find Tommy." Her eyes rose to meet his. "Max, Jacob Freeman is dead."

Chapter Twenty-Four

Max and Theresa drove around all the shops and fast-food restaurants within reasonable biking distance of the Freeman home, showing the pictures of Jacob and Tommy. So far, they'd come up dry. A couple people at the department stores remembered seeing Jacob, but having no jobs available, he'd left, apparently to continue his search.

By now it was late evening. They'd spent the entire day asking questions without coming up with any answers. Parking by the Brewery, they decided to walk back to Theresa's place, taking those few moments to unwind.

Max mentioned dinner, but Theresa declined, not really hungry and feeling a bit saddened at their lack of progress. She felt in her heart it was already too late to help Jacob, but Tommy could still be rescued, if they could just get the right answer to the right question.

Within a few minutes, they were in the heart of the French Quarter, the sounds of jazz spilling out into the streets from the clubs located up and down Charters and Bourbon Streets, catcalls echoing in the darkness from the sex clubs. A cool breeze carried the unique scents of New Orleans. Smells of magnolia and honeysuckle, faint and seductive, intermingled with the spicy aroma of Creole cooking and the salty brine wafting from the waters of the nearby river basin. These were the scents of home.

Turning the corner onto Theresa's street, Max reached down and grasped her hand, wrapping it in his warm grip, squeezing her fingers gently. Raising their entwined hands, he pressed a kiss to her fingers. With just a few more steps, they reached her door.

Theresa stared into his eyes. In their depths she read his sadness. Not finding Tommy was eating him up. He tried to portray a stoic, guarded persona, to show the events playing out around him didn't affect him, but she knew the real Max. He was hurting, and when he hurt, she hurt, too.

Sliding the key into the lock, she opened the door and walked inside, tugging him behind her. She didn't switch on any lights but left the room awash in semi-darkness with just enough lights from the street beyond to be able to see. She flipped the lock and led him forward, through the store and up the stairs to her apartment.

Reaching the top step she turned to him, placed her trembling hands on his chest and met his gaze squarely. Her fingertips played with a button on the front of his shirt, plucking at it with her nails.

"Stay with me tonight. I need you." Her voice came out in a sultry whisper, and the catch in Max's breath told her he'd heard.

"I need you too, baby." His hands reached out to cup her face, tilting it upward as his head descended and his lips met hers softly. Just a brush, butterfly-soft, at first. He pulled back and looked into her eyes. They drifted closed, her lips slightly parted as his lips met hers hungrily, devouring hers, deepening the kiss. When she opened her eyes, she was awed at the want and need in his. But more, at the love reflected in their depths.

"Make love to me. Help me forget today." She pulled his head down to close the distance between them. Claiming his lips in a demanding kiss, her tongue dueled with his in a seductive game of mastery they were both determined to win.

His hands speared into her hair, his lips never leaving hers, wet and sucking, a kiss filled with his own need. Pulling back slightly, he voiced his request.

"Take your hair down for me, baby. I love to run my fingers through it. It's so amazingly sexy."

Reaching up, Theresa pulled the long braid over her shoulder and took out the elastic band holding the ends together. Twining her fingers through its mass, she separated the long strands until they were free, flowing down her back to fall to her hips.

With a shy inviting smile, she turned and walked through the open doorway to her bedroom, beckoning for him to follow.

Max's footsteps sounded with a brisk clip-clop, his boots echoing against the hardwood floor. Its deep golden color glowed in the diffused light of a lamp she'd left on earlier. Max had never been in Theresa's bedroom before tonight.

Curiosity had him glancing around, taking in the white cast-iron bedstead, the intricate scrollwork accented with touches of burnished gold at the knobbed balls on the four corners. An embroidered deep royal-purple bedspread and pillows adorned the bed. It was so much like Theresa. Regal, unique, strong and ever so valuable.

Her face looked uncertain, watching him the way a mouse watches a cat, anticipating the pounce.

"If you've changed your mind, baby, I'll go. You never have to do anything you don't want to."

"No, it's not that." She collapsed to sit on the side of the bed, all that glorious hair fanning out behind her. "I was just thinking I didn't want to push you into something you don't want. We weren't looking to start anything when this all began. Just the opposite, we avoided each other. I don't know where this will all end when my job with you is over."

Max sat next to her on the decadent purple velvet. "You're right, we don't know where this is headed. I just have one question." He stared deeply and directly into her eyes. "Do you care about me?"

Without hesitation she answered him. "Yes, Max, I care about you."

"I care about you, too. Things are unsettled right now. Once this case is over, we can see where this is leading. I made mistakes before—we both have—and I don't want to make those same mistakes again."

Theresa nodded her head. "Okay, let's take things slowly, not rush into anything." She raised her hand up, cupping his cheek. "Are you going to stay with me tonight? I still want you to make love to me."

Max grinned. "Oh, yeah, I'm staying."

Chapter Twenty-Five

Theresa awoke to Remy's impatient knocking on the back door. Max had stumbled from her bed before dawn, with plans to head over to his ransacked office. Since the police were finished in there, he wanted to look for leads on Tommy and Jacob Freeman.

Remy looked like he'd been dragged out of bed himself. Max must have called him before he'd left, to make sure she had a babysitter. She wasn't too worried about the anonymous threat in that note. Still, she'd agreed to let them watch over her until things calmed down.

"Morning, Remy. Coffee's not ready yet, it's too early. Give me a minute, and I'll get it started."

He walked to the counter holding the half-filled coffee maker, before he gave a groaning sigh. *Must have been a long night.* She wondered who he'd been with this time. Remy loved women, enjoyed their company and spent most of his free time dating.

"Hope you had a good time last night," she teased, watching him stretch, his tall, lean frame accented by the jeans and T-shirt, muscles rippling. It was easy to understand what all those women saw in him. He was a friendly, funny and very sexy man.

Remy grinned, perfect white teeth revealed in his smile. "Oh, yeah, it was great. How was your night?"

Heat rushed into her cheeks and she felt the blush spread across them. He obviously knew Max had spent the night. "It was wonderful."

"Wonderful? I didn't think Max could inspire wonderful."

"You'd be surprised at just how *inspiring* he can be," she quipped, moving gracefully to the counter with the coffee paraphernalia. Soon the fragrant aroma filled the kitchen.

"Things seem to be going well between you. Have you told him how you feel?" Remy's question caught her off-guard.

"We've decided to just take things day by day until this whole case has been resolved." Suddenly nervous about standing there in her nightclothes when Remy was fully dressed, she reached down and tightened the belt on her robe. "I'm just going to run upstairs and get dressed."

Remy glanced at her, obviously confused by the nervousness in her tone. She'd been around him many times when she was still in her nightclothes. But that was before she started sleeping with his brother.

"Hang on a second." Reaching into his back pocket, Remy pulled out several folded sheets of paper, showing them to Theresa. "Jacob Freeman's parents found a journal tucked under the mattress in Jacob's bedroom." He shrugged at Theresa's wide-eyed stare. "Apparently they didn't even know he kept one. Mr. Freeman called Max and he had me stop by there this morning. They gave me the last few pages." Unfolding the wrinkled sheets, he laid them on the table.

Theresa stared at the journal pages. She lowered herself onto a chair, mentally and physically stiffening her spine before reaching out to pick them up. Instantly images swirled in her mind's eye, coalescing and focusing to a crisp vision.

She saw Jacob walk through the sliding doors of a familiar-looking hardware store, striding briskly to the customer service counter. He spoke with the man working the counter, filling out what she assumed was a job application. They spoke animatedly for several more minutes before Jacob turned to leave. He had a big grin on his face as he exited the store.

The image faded and Theresa laid the papers on the table.

"We need to call Max. I got a vision of Jacob at a hardware store. It looked like that really big one over in Metairie. We need to get over there, show his picture. Somebody there will remember him."

"I know that place. Tell you what, you get changed. We'll drive over and call Max from there if we get some concrete information, okay?"

Theresa paced back and forth between the table and the counter, mumbling to herself, until Remy caught her by the elbow, stopping her in her tracks.

"It's early. They aren't even open yet. You can call Maggie, have her come watch the store and we'll go. I've got Jacob's picture in my car."

He gently pushed on her shoulders, pointing her toward

the stairs. "Go. Dress."

Within minutes, Theresa was back downstairs. "Let's go now." She was anxious yet eager.

"I'll call Maggie from the car. We have to hurry, Remy. I don't know why but I feel a real sense of urgency. We have to go now."

The Homefront Hardware Store was a massive, do-it-yourself, home-and-garden supply center, doing its best to compete with the huge conglomerates taking over all the mom-and-pop hardware stores in southern Louisiana. Having been owned and operated by the same family for more than twenty years, it was a place where clerks knew their regulars by name. The bustling crowds pushed their loaded shopping carts up and down the well-stocked aisles, a testament to the loyalty of their customer base.

One of the things Remy and Theresa were counting on was that somebody there would remember talking to Jacob. Theresa knew the two cases were connected. Whoever killed Jacob was the same person who had Tommy. In her mind it had become a case of *find Jacob, find Tommy.*

She walked at a brisk pace, with Remy close behind her, through the big automated doors and straight to the customer service counter.

"Excuse me. I need to speak with someone who was here on Thursday." Theresa locked eyes with the harried, stooped, gray-haired gentleman behind the counter. His bright blue apron proudly proclaimed My Name is Eddie. Eddie flipped through the pages of a catalog, dividing his attention between it and the computer keyboard, busily typing information into the system and ignoring Theresa.

"I said, excuse me, Eddie. I need to speak with somebody who was here Thursday afternoon. This is a police matter." Eddie's head popped up.

"You a cop?"

Remy reached around from behind Theresa, shoving his badge in Eddie's face. "I am. Now answer the lady's question."

"Okay, okay, hold on. I need to get the schedule. What day did you say again?" Eddie walked several feet away, down the massive counter, past the computers and the cash register, to a clipboard hanging on a hook by the last cubicle. He grabbed it and hurried back, flipping through the pages as he walked.

"Thursday…what time?"

"It would have been afternoon, probably after three o'clock. Is there somebody here today who was working then?" Theresa tried to remain calm, but again that sense of urgency, the need to rush, grew stronger.

"Let's see. Pete, Chuck and Juan were all here Thursday afternoon. Juan and Chuck won't be in until two o'clock this afternoon. Pete's back in shipping now, though. Straight back, through the flooring department, next to the big double doors. You can't miss it—"

"Thanks, Eddie, we appreciate your help," Remy broke in.

Nearly running, they made their way toward the back,

past the flooring department and through the double doors. One lone man was loading a long cart with lighting materials, boxes filled with lamps, ceiling fans, and lamping accessories. Theresa and Remy walked over. She felt a momentary letdown when she read the name on his apron. Franklyn.

"Hello, Franklyn. We're looking for Pete. Eddie at customer service said he was back here. Could we speak to him?" Theresa tried to make her tone sound crisp and official.

Franklyn stopped stacking his cart, reaching up with his right hand to scratch at his smooth-shaven bald pate.

"Pete. He just clocked out. Went home sick. If you hurry, you might catch him in the parkin' lot out back," Franklyn offered. "Anything I can help you folks with?"

"No, thanks. We need to speak with Pete." Remy shook his head. "Which is the quickest exit to the back parking area?"

Franklyn gestured to his left, toward a marked exit sign conveniently located by the loading dock.

Remy turned to Theresa. "Go back up front and get Pete's address from Eddie, just in case I don't catch him." When she started to protest, he interjected, "If we argue about this, we may not catch him at all. I'll meet you out front, either way. Now go."

Theresa watched for a moment as Remy sprinted toward the door, swinging it open and was gone within seconds. She quickly made her way back to the front, to finagle Pete's address. It took a good bit of arm-twisting, but in the end,

Eddie complied and gave her the address.

She walked through the automated front doors, scanning the parking lot for Remy. His blue Impala pulled up adjacent to where she stood, and the passenger door swung open. Remy leaned toward her and motioned for her to get in.

"Did you get the address?" Remy peeled out of the parking lot.

"Yes. It's 1723 Sycamore Drive."

"Okay, I know where that is. It's only a couple of minutes from here. Get that seatbelt buckled up."

Pete lived in a single-story ranch-style house, its white walls and chocolate-brown shutters clean and pristine, looking newly painted. The hedges lining the front walkway were clipped to a precise angle, green and healthy-appearing. There wasn't a car parked in the driveway. Not a good sign.

"Here he comes now," Theresa said. Moments later a dark blue Jeep pulled into the driveway and a middle-aged, dark-haired man stepped from it. He walked over to them, his bearing straight, posture rigid.

"Can I help you folks?" His look encompassed both Theresa and Remy, but he wasn't forthcoming in his welcome. Lines of pain were evident around his eyes and across his forehead.

"Pete?" He nodded, his eyes narrowing.

"My name's Theresa Crawford and this is Remy Lamoreaux." Remy pulled out his badge, showing it to Pete.

"Were you at work at Homefront Hardware on Thursday afternoon, between three and closing time?"

Pete nodded again, so she hurried on.

"Did a young man come in inquiring about work? His name is Jacob Freeman." She detected the almost imperceptible shifting of his stance, enough to know she was on the right track.

"Why do you want to know?"

"Pete, Jacob's parents are concerned because he hasn't been seen since Thursday afternoon. He never came home, so we're trying to help find him." Theresa kept her voice calm, and Remy stood back, letting her do the talking. She knew he'd jump in, if it was necessary, but right now, he was letting her ease into things. He was the cop, but this was unofficial, so he was letting her run with it.

"There was a young kid, came in about four-thirty, asking about work. Seemed a nice enough guy. Willing to do anything. We didn't have anything, though. With the Christmas season ready to start, the store's been hiring full out for the past few weeks, and we've an overabundance of people right now. That's what I told the kid."

"Did he say anything about where he might go after he left your store?"

Pete shrugged. "I kind of gave the kid a lead on somebody who might have a job. He seemed real anxious to find something, so I told him about a couple of roofing jobs I'd filled an order for. Told him to check with the guy doing the jobs, see if he could use the extra help." Pete shifted nervously from foot to foot.

Theresa looked at Remy, and he nodded for her to go ahead and ask.

"Pete, we need you to give us all the information you

gave Jacob about the roofing job. Where did you send him, who did you tell him to contact? Please, it's very important. This person may be able to help us track Jacob down and help get him home."

Tingles ran down Theresa's spine. *This was it.* She knew it, felt it to her marrow. This was the missing piece of the puzzle they needed to find the boys, both Tommy and Jacob.

"Company's called Black's Back to Basics. I sent him to see the guy who owns it, Steven Black."

Chapter Twenty-Six

Max had a bad feeling in his gut all day. He couldn't shake it. As a cop that same intuition had saved his ass more than once. Now it was pestering him, like an itch he couldn't scratch.

Taking one hand off the wheel, he grabbed his cell phone and dialed Theresa's shop. It rang a couple of times and Maggie picked up.

"Hey, Maggie, it's Max Lamoreaux. Could I speak with Theresa please?"

"Sorry, Theresa's not here. She called early this morning and asked me to cover the shop for her again."

"Did she say where she could be reached?" That antsy feeling was starting to work overtime now, gnawing at him.

"No, sir. She and Remy took off before I got here."

She's with Remy. He gave a sigh of relief. Max dialed Remy's number and got his voice mail. Leaving an abrupt message instructing him to call him back right away, he snapped the phone shut.

It had been a frustrating morning, dealing with the local New Orleans cops about his ransacked office. They'd told him the threatening note had been constructed on site, out of his own newspapers and magazines. Dozens of sets of fingerprints were found throughout the office, but only two sets on the letter. His and one other. They hadn't come up with a match yet, but were still working. Max knew it would be a dead end.

Where the hell are Remy and Theresa? When he'd left her this morning, crawling out of that warm comfortable bed, she had been sleeping so peacefully. She looked so breathtakingly beautiful, curled on her side, her long blond hair sprawled out around her, one perfect pink breast peeking out from beneath the bedspread. It had taken all his resolve to walk away when he'd rather have crawled back into the bed and made her his again. The need to be with her, to make her understand she was his just as he belonged to her, pushed at him. Instead, he had called Remy to watch over her, and went to work.

Every instinct he had, both as a P.I. and an ex-cop, told him Tommy was running out of time.

He glanced over at the folder lying on the passenger seat. Although there was no proof, he believed Theresa when she said that Jacob's and Tommy's cases were somehow connected. Right now the only thing linking the two was the fact they attended the same high school. He'd checked with the school first thing this morning, but they hadn't had any of the same classes, even though they were both in the same grade. Nothing in the last two years showed they'd ever had a single class together.

His phone rang and he peered at the caller ID. "Hey, bro. Where the hell are you and Theresa? You were supposed to stay put."

"Well, good morning to you, too. Theresa had an idea of a place to look for Jacob. We hit pay dirt, buddy."

"Where? What?"

"Homefront Hardware Store. Apparently Jacob Freeman was in Thursday afternoon asking about a job. Talked to a guy named Pete. This Pete tells Jacob about a contractor who has two roofing jobs lined up, ready to start. Said he should check with this guy, maybe he'd have something for him."

"Who'd he send him to?" Max's stomach clenched, his hand tightening on the wheel. *Please, God, let this be it.*

"Guy named Steven Black. We're on our way over there right now."

"No, wait—"

"We're already pulling up in front of Black's house. I'll call you if we find out anything. Keep your phone on." With that, Remy hung up.

Steven Black. Max's mind mulled over that. Bit by bit, it started to add up. Theresa said whoever picked up Tommy was somebody he knew. Steven fit. She said he'd been picked up by a large white vehicle, probably a van. Steven drove a white pickup truck, which was close. He'd talked to Steven at the Saunders's house, but the man could have been lying to him the whole time. Now, Jacob had gone to see Steven, and he'd gone missing, too.

Grabbing up his phone, he dialed the NOPD. Fortunately, somebody owed him favors. He was calling one in.

"Morning, Bill. It's Lamoreaux. I need you to check the DMV for me, see how many vehicles are registered to a

Steven Black. Might be under his personal name or it may be under the name of his business, Black's Back to Basics. Specifically, check to see if he has a white van."

"Man, come on. I don't have time for this," Bill whined over the phone line.

"Look, you owe me. This is an emergency. Call me on my cell as soon as you get anything."

"Is this about your missing godson?"

"It might be. Put a rush on it, okay?" Giving Bill his cell number, Max hung up, again running the facts through his mind. It all added up, made sense. The question was why? Steven Black was a well-respected contractor in the New Orleans area. Lots of people used his services. As far as Max knew, he was clean, didn't have a record. There had to be a reason.

Once he figured that out, he'd be one step closer to finding Tommy and hopefully Jacob Freeman, too.

Remy parked his car beside the red brick wall in front of Steven Black's house. Two large stone columns, topped by lanterns on either side, flanked the driveway. A well-maintained yard, spectacular bushes and trees highlighted the view.

Theresa sat silently, her eyes closed. She was tense, her body so stiff she practically vibrated. Remy had been around her long enough, he was familiar with scenes similar to this. She knew he'd wait until she was ready to speak.

Moments later, she exhaled a whisper of breath and

opened her eyes. Her hands rubbed up and down her arms, smoothing the goose bumps covering the chilled flesh of her forearms. Her eyes glimmered with unshed tears as she turned to face Remy.

"He was here. He left his bike right there, leaning against that column when he went to talk with Mr. Black. I saw him walk up to the front door and knock. He waited for a few minutes, then stepped off the front porch and went to that window." She pointed at the large window to the right of the front door.

"I saw him look in and then he walked back toward his bicycle. Something, a noise maybe, stopped him and he walked around the side of the house instead." She paused, squinting as if trying to see something in the distance before continuing.

"There were two vehicles parked in the driveway. One was a white pickup truck with a company logo on the side. The other one was…a white van."

"A white van? Like the one you saw pick up Tommy from the side of the road?"

Theresa nodded, raising trembling fingers to her lips.

"I'm calling Max back." Remy reached for the phone clipped to his belt.

"No, wait. We need to do what we came here to do. Let's go talk to Mr. Black about Jacob."

Opening the car door, Theresa clambered out before Remy could stop her. "Dammit," he muttered, following silently.

They walked across the manicured lawn to the front

porch, and he rapped on the door. No answer. Glancing back toward the empty drive, Remy remarked, "He's probably not home." He pointed. "No cars, trucks, vans or anything else in the driveway. We're going to have to come back later."

Theresa's shoulders slumped dejectedly. She wanted this whole thing over. The strain of this case was showing on everyone she loved.

She felt like time was running out. Events were soon going to come to a head. There was danger coming—she sensed it. Somebody was going to be hurt, possibly killed. Who it would be was still dark to her, but it was going to happen soon. God help them all stay safe, she prayed.

Chapter Twenty-Seven

"I've got an idea."

They were seated in Remy's Impala, parked in front of Steven Black's house. He reached for his cell phone and dialed Information.

"I'd like the number for a business listing. Black's Back to Basics."

After a few seconds, the recording came back. "That number is 555-6759."

Remy dialed. Expecting voice mail to pick up, he straightened when the phone was answered.

"Black's Back to Basics. This is Steven Black."

"Mr. Black, my name's Remington. I'd like to get an estimate for some interior work I need done. I've heard good things about your work. Can we meet? I'd like to get started as soon as possible."

Remy glanced over at Theresa, and saw her nod of approval.

"Mr. Remington, I've got kind of a full schedule right now with jobs already lined up. Exactly how soon would you need this work done?"

"The wife's been after me to remodel the kitchen for months. She's going out of town tomorrow, and I want to get this done while she's gone. I'd need you to start immediately. I'm willing to pay extra for the inconvenience." Remy's voice spun the lie so smoothly, there wasn't a hitch in his tone to reveal his deception. He listened to the hesitation at the other end, and knew Black was considering his offer.

"Okay, Mr. Remington, why don't we meet someplace and we can talk about the work you want done. Where would be convenient for you?"

"Actually right now I'm over at Homefront Hardware. That's where I got your name, from one of their employees." *Always best to stick with the truth when you can.* "He said that you live close by. Maybe we could meet at your home?"

Again there was silence on the other end. "Sure, that'd be okay. I can be there in about fifteen minutes. Do you need the address?"

"Yes, that would be great."

After getting the address from Steven, Remy hung up the phone. He leaned his head back against the headrest of the seat and closed his eyes.

"He'll be here in about fifteen minutes." He craned his head around, opening his eyes. "I'm going to suggest something, and you're not going to like it, but I'm saying it anyway. Before he gets here, I want you to climb in the back and stay out of sight."

Theresa opened her mouth to protest.

"I know you don't like it, but that's tough. He's seen you before with Max. He could recognize you and that would blow the whole thing."

"He won't recognize me, Remy. He barely got a glance at

me before."

"We can't take that chance. If he's involved in this, he may be the one who left the note. Let me handle this. We're just here to ask questions about Jacob."

★　★　★

Theresa paused, considering her words. "Remy, it's more than just Jacob. Somehow, someway, he's connected with Tommy, too. Be very careful, but see if you can ask him about both boys."

"Okay, I'll ask. Just please, stay out of sight until I've talked to him. I've done this before you know." He smiled at her and gave her an exaggerated wink. "I'm a professional."

Shaking her head, she opened the car door and climbed onto the back seat, hunkering down as far as possible. Before too much time passed, she heard a vehicle pull into the drive and the engine shut off.

She heard Remy's door open and close, and the murmur of voices faded as the two men walked away from the car. She held her breath, saying a quick prayer Remy would find out something about the boys.

Hopeful they would find Tommy soon, deep down she knew it was already too late for Jacob. The most they could do would be to find his body so his parents could gain some type of closure. It wouldn't be enough, but it was all they could offer.

Unable to resist the temptation any longer, she raised her head up just enough to peer out the car window. Remy and Mr. Black were nowhere in sight.

Sitting a little farther up, she could see the very end of a white vehicle protruding through the brick-and-concrete posts lining the drive. What could it hurt if she snuck over and touched it? Maybe she could get something off it, it was worth a shot.

She opened the car door as quietly as possible, making her way outside and pushing it almost all the way closed, leaving it cracked the tiniest bit to avoid any noise.

Her head swung back and forth as she walked, glancing around to see if anybody had spotted her. So far she was in the clear. She jogged toward the end of the drive. Parked there was an older white panel van. The only windows were on the driver's and passenger's front doors. The back was completely enclosed.

This van looked eerily familiar. Tentatively she reached out, fingertips barely touching the cool metal of the rear cargo door.

Scenes screamed through her brain. Her knees buckled. Pictures of Tommy and Steven loading Tommy's Suzuki into the back, the flat tire evident as they rolled it inside. Tommy and Steven on the drive toward New Orleans, talking about school and work, his parents, casual chitchat between acquaintances.

She jerked her hand away from the metal as though it were fiery hot. *He was the one! Steven Black had taken Tommy!*

"Oh, God," she whispered, "Remy's inside that house with a madman, and he doesn't know it!" She didn't have a phone, no way of contacting him or Max. What was she going to do?

Max grabbed his cell phone on the first ring, not bothering to check the caller ID. His heart raced when he heard his friend's voice from the police station.

"You've got good instincts, as always, Lamoreaux," Bill drawled. "Steven Black owns two vehicles, one Ford F250 pickup truck and one Chevy Astro van. Both vehicles are registered under his name to his business. That what you needed?"

"Thanks, bud, I owe you one." He hung up. Every one of his instincts screamed this was it. Steven Black knew something. *Damn, why hasn't Remy called back yet?*

He knew Remy was a good cop and could handle himself, but Theresa—she was a wildcard. Besides, how hard could it be to ask a few questions about a missing kid? Either he'd seen Jacob or he hadn't. One way or another, they'd have answers soon.

Making a sharp U-turn, Max slammed his foot down on the gas pedal and sped toward Steven Black's house. "The hell with waiting, I'm going over there."

Remy sat in Steven's living room, his sharp cop's eyes taking in every detail, cataloging the scene for future reference. It was a longstanding habit. His instincts pulsated, demanding he pay close attention to every detail.

Steven Black walked back into the room carrying two

glasses of iced tea, handing one to Remy before setting the other down on the coffee table, and took a seat.

"What's this job about, Mr. Remington? You mentioned something about a kitchen remodel?"

Remy set down his glass before reaching into his shirt pocket for Jacob's picture. "Actually, Mr. Black, that was a bit of subterfuge on my part. I'm actually here looking into the case of a missing teenager."

Black's body stiffened immediately at his words. Remy watched Steven closely. His years on the force had made him skilled at reading body language, and any fool could see that this guy had something to hide. Remy was nobody's fool.

"You lied? Why? I don't know anything about a missing boy."

Remy's pulse rate sped up at that. He hadn't specified the missing teenager was a *boy. Just take it slow, maybe we're getting somewhere here.*

"Mr. Black, would you mind looking at a picture for me? Tell me if you've seen this person before."

"Sure, no problem," he answered.

Remy handed Jacob's picture to him, still watching, gauging his reactions. Steven's fingers visibly trembled as he stared at the photo of Jacob. His shock was evident. Remy didn't doubt he recognized Jacob.

"I don't think so. Maybe, I don't know. These teenagers nowadays, they all look the same to me." Steven tried to cover, blustering over his response. His eyes darted around the living room, never making eye contact.

"Mr. Black, I was told by an employee at Homefront

Hardware that he suggested this young man come see you about a job." Steven Black winced slightly, but still kept his mouth shut. *Probably a good thing. This guy definitely isn't a good liar.*

"Nope, nobody has talked to me about a job. Actually, I wish he had. I've got two roofing contracts coming up and need some part-time help."

"Mr. Black. We know he was here. We have a witness that saw Jacob stop at your house on Thursday afternoon and park his bicycle outside your drive." Remy calmly stated this falsehood. The only witness he had was Theresa, who had seen it in a vision. It was a stab in the dark, but he was going to try it anyway.

"Somebody saw him here? No, no. That can't be right. He wasn't here I tell you. I never saw him." Steven's voice rose, his words tumbling over themselves. He stood, hands on his hips, staring at Remy.

"Who are you, anyway, to be asking me all the questions, mister?"

Remy smiled, reaching into his pants pocket, and pulled out his identification. "Detective Remington Lamoreaux. I'm with the New Orleans Police Department."

Remy could swear that Steven Black's eyes nearly rolled back in his head, all color leaching from his face. He was as white as a sheet, trembling.

"He wasn't here. That's all I got to say. You go, right now."

"Steven, you're lying to me. We know he was here. I want to know where he was going after he left."

"And I'm telling you, I don't care what your witnesses say, I didn't see that kid." Stalking to the door, Steven swung it open wide. His face, pale earlier, now flushed red. Beads of sweat formed on his forehead as he stood there, visibly trembling. Remy wanted to push him for answers, but was afraid the guy would have a heart attack right there in the foyer and they'd never find either kid.

"Mr. Black, are you feeling okay? You're looking ill. Do you need me to contact somebody for you or call 9-1-1?"

"No! Really, I'm fine. I'm just tired, been working too many jobs recently. I guess I need to take it easier, slow down a bit." Steven reached up with one hand and wiped at the beads of sweat dotting his forehead.

Remy glanced through the open doorway and groaned silently. Theresa was clearly visible standing next to the van parked in the drive. If Black glanced that way, he might recognize her.

"Thank you for your cooperation. We'll be in touch if there are further questions." Remy stood, prepared to leave when an open doorway to the right caught his gaze. Shiny and gleaming, the front rim of a bicycle could be seen. Metallic red paint glinted when the light hit the front bumper, and Remy's brain shifted into overdrive. He knew Jacob had ridden his bike here, but nobody had mentioned the color. Had it been red?

Maybe his imagination was running amok. Maybe it was Steven's bicycle. If it was, though, why was it inside the house?

He continued toward the door, hoping that Steven

hadn't noticed his diverted attention. He'd almost made it, when the door swung closed with a slam. Steven stood barring his way.

"You couldn't just mind your own business, could you? You had to come snooping around here, asking stupid questions. As if that's not bad enough, no, you had to be nosy, looking around and seeing things you don't need to see."

Steven took three steps away from the door and reached into the drawer of a wooden desk. His hand emerged holding a pistol. Looking at it, Remy recognized it right away as a .38 caliber. Definitely big enough to do a lot of damage, especially at this close range.

"You don't want to do this. I'm a cop. I showed you my identification. Threatening a cop is a serious thing."

Remy kept his voice calm, matter-of-fact, when just the opposite was true. Even off-duty he had a weapon with him, out of sight in an ankle holster. He cursed silently, wishing he could get to it, but he knew Black had the drop on him and would shoot him before he made it halfway to his weapon. He blamed himself for not telling Max to meet him here.

"That kid wasn't supposed to come here. Nobody *ever* comes here. That's why this place is so perfect for me. I can be alone. But that kid, he was going to ruin everything."

"What was he going to ruin?"

"He saw too much. He came around the side of the house and saw us arguing." Steven raised the hand not holding the gun up to the side of his head, rubbing at his temple. He stared at Remy, glassy-eyed with pain.

Something was up. But what? "Who were you arguing with, Steven?"

"Who…oh, I was arguing with Tommy. We're always arguing lately." He said it nonchalantly, emotionless, yet Remy's pulse rate trip-hammered, his heartbeat slamming against his ribcage.

Steven has Tommy.

"Are we talking about Tommy Saunders?"

Steven looked at him in surprise. "Of course we're talking about Tommy Saunders. Things were almost finished, and that Jacob person saw us and almost ruined everything." Steven waved the gun around dramatically, gesturing with his hands, as if he had forgotten he was holding it. "He kept screaming he was going to call the police. I had to stop him, you see that don't you? I wasn't ready yet. It was just too soon."

Remy couldn't believe what he heard. Although rambling, Steven had basically confessed to taking Tommy and, worse, having done something to the Freeman kid. He needed to keep him talking.

Outside the front window he caught a glimpse of long blond hair surrounding a pale face and wide blue eyes peering through the sliver of an opening in the drapes. Theresa. Dammit, she'd ruin everything if she came any closer. He needed to keep Steven distracted and talking.

"Too soon for what, Steven? What happened to Jacob and Tommy?" His tone soothing, Remy asked the question in a way to encourage Steven's rambling discourse.

"My plans. I had everything worked out, you see. Tommy was perfect. I knew he would be. That other boy, he was going to ruin everything. I had to shut him up. I had to make him stop." Once again Steven rubbed at his temple with his empty hand. His face was bright red, his breathing erratic.

"What plans, Steven? What part does Tommy play in all this?"

Steven stared at Remy, his eyes widening. Remy knew he finally comprehended what was happening, and that he'd said too much.

"Time's up now, I guess. Things are mostly in place. I'll just have to accelerate ahead of schedule and pray everything works out."

Steven's expression softened. A look of sympathy crossed his face.

"Mr. Lamoreaux, you seem like a decent fellow, and I'm sure you're a fine police officer. I'm really sorry."

Remy stood frozen in place, his eyes never faltering from the gun. "Sorry?"

Steven nodded his head, the gun still pointed at Remy's chest. "Yes, I'm sorry," he said, as his finger squeezed the trigger.

Chapter Twenty-Eight

A shrill scream escaped from the back of Theresa's throat as the retort of the gunshot broke the afternoon quiet. Moments before, she'd stood outside the living room window, hands cupped around either side of her face, blocking the afternoon glare. Peering in the open slit between the curtain panels, she'd hoped to signal Remy to get out. Ever since touching the van, her psychic sense had been screeching warnings to leave. To run. Danger flooded her senses, the acrid taste of fear overwhelming, a bilious lump in her gut.

Her fear turned to outrage as Remy clutched his chest. Bright red bloomed between his fingers, spilling through them to fall in crimson droplets speckling the hardwood. Everything played out in slow motion. Remy's gaze met hers through the panes of glass. She could read the shock and pain. He seemed to fold inward, collapsing to the floor, still and unmoving.

"No, Remy. Please, no." Stumbling backward, she raced up the porch steps and flung open the door. The living room was empty. Steven was gone. Theresa heard the slam of a door in the distance but didn't care. Remy lay motionless. The strong metallic scent of blood hovered in the air.

Dropping to her knees beside him, she prayed as she felt for a heartbeat. She felt a slow, jittery pulse in the side of his neck, watched the imperceptible rise and fall of his chest with each labored breath. She heard the shallow, wheezing inhalation, a gurgling wet sound in his throat. *Thank you, God, he's still alive.*

With trembling fingers, she managed to unclip his cell phone from his belt and dialed 9-1-1.

"I need an ambulance and the police! A police officer has been shot!"

"An officer has been shot?"

"Yes, dammit. Remy Lamoreaux." The phone nestled between her ear and shoulder, she applied pressure one-handed to the wound, as instructed by the dispatcher. She rattled off Steven's address.

"We have a rescue vehicle and police dispatched to your location." The calming voice of the dispatcher echoed in Theresa's ears. In the distance the wailing sound of sirens was faint but drawing closer. She knew help was on the way.

"Hold on, Remy. The ambulance is almost here." Guilt ate at her. If only she had known sooner Steven Black was the person who'd caused so much heartache and pain. Her head jerked up at a noise by the front door.

"What the hell happened?" Max rushed in, dropping to one knee beside his prostrate brother, his hand reaching to check for a pulse.

"Steven Black shot him. The police and an ambulance are on the way." Her gaze drifted back to Remy, to her hands pressing down on his chest. Dark red blood continued to bubble between her fingers, warm and sticky. Bending forward slightly, she increased the pressure, before looking back up at Max.

"Steven's the one, Max."

"What? Dammit, I knew I should have stopped you two from coming here on your own. You should have waited until I got here."

Max yanked his shirt free from his pants, and tore the buttons loose as he dragged it over his shoulders and free of his body. Haphazardly wadding it up, he moved Theresa's bloody hands aside and pressed the cloth against the gaping bullet wound.

"Hold that down as firm as you can, we've got to control the bleeding until the paramedics get here." He brushed a hand through his brother's dark hair. Bending low, he whispered, "Hold on, bro. You stay strong and fight, damn you, fight."

"Max?" Remy's voice was faint, so weak it chilled Max to the bone.

"Yeah, bro, it's me."

"Steven's…the guy…" Remy's voice trailed off as he coughed, a trickle of blood coursing from the corner of his mouth.

"Yeah, I got it. We'll catch the son of a bitch and he's going to rot in prison."

"He's the one who took Tommy…" Remy's head lolled back, unconscious.

Max's roar was drowned out by the sound of sirens as the paramedics pulled into the drive. Rushing inside, they began working on Remy. He lay so still and silent now, Max's heart ached. He couldn't lose his brother, not like this.

"Where is that bastard?" Max wheeled around and stalked over to Theresa, who stood by the front doorway, her eyes huge, watching the paramedics working on his brother. Blood stains splattered her clothes, her hands covered with Remy's blood.

"I don't know, Max. I was standing outside." Theresa gestured toward the drapes. "I heard some of what was said, though. He admitted to killing Jacob Freeman because he was going to tell the police that Steven had kidnapped Tommy."

"God, I don't believe this. That lousy, good for nothing, worthless piece of filth. He worked for Tommy's family. Why would he do this?" Turning away from Theresa, Max slammed his fist into the wall. Drywall dust drifted outward from the hole he caused.

Inhaling a deep breath, Max fought to rein in his temper. Turning away from the sight of his brother lying bleeding and helpless on the floor, he reached for Theresa, pulling her close.

Theresa laid her head on his shoulder, and he felt her arms wrap tightly around his back.

He held Theresa as the paramedics carefully loaded Remy onto a gurney and wheeled him to the door. Strapped down, IV tubes running into his arm, Remy made the rough trip over the rocky driveway and to the waiting ambulance.

Max jogged alongside his brother, whispering encouragement.

★ ★ ★

Theresa followed behind at a slower pace, giving him a few moments with his brother, some private time. Tears rolled down her cheeks as the ambulance pulled away from the curb, its sirens wailing out their mournful tones.

"Dear God, please watch out for Remy. Keep him safe. Please," she prayed.

Max reached forward and wrapped his arms tightly around her. She reached around him, squeezing back.

Theresa hid her face against his chest, inhaling the warm masculine scent that was singularly Max. Reaching up, she wiped at the tears trickling in a slow cascade down her cheeks.

"Do you know where Steven went, babe? Did you hear or see anything?"

She shook her head. "By the time I'd opened the front door, he was gone. He must have gone out the back."

"Excuse me, are you Max Lamoreaux?" A uniformed officer stood beside Max, awaiting his answer.

"Yes. What do you need, officer?"

"Sir, we've got a bit of a situation here. If you could come with me, please."

Armed police officers, outfitted with multiple weapons, handguns and rifles, scrambled around them. The entire area was a beehive of activity as police car after police car pulled up, with men and women spilling into the melee.

"What's going on?" Max's tone demanded answers. His eyes widened at the sight of a SWAT van pulling up, barricades being erected on the street to block oncoming traffic.

They walked a short distance to a police cruiser, where a suited gentleman, obviously the senior person in charge, barked out orders. The officers rapidly responded, taking up positions alongside the house and on the other side of the cement block fence lining the side of the driveway.

As a former cop, Max knew marksman positioning when he saw it. The situation had clearly gone to hell in a hand-basket.

The officer who had led them over spoke quietly to the man in charge, gesturing briefly at Max and Theresa, before walking beyond the driveway to join the other officers lining the front fence.

"Mr. Lamoreaux, my name's Wheeler. Your brother's a fine officer and a good man. We're all praying for him."

"Thank you, sir. What's the status on Steven Black? I assume you've heard something." Max gestured toward the high police presence surrounding them. Another uniformed officer walked up and handed Max a light blue T-shirt. Max nodded his thanks and shrugged his muscular shoulders into the loaner shirt. "This is more than an officer down situation. What have you got?"

"Mr. Lamoreaux, shortly after the 9-1-1 came in, a second call was placed from this location. It was Black. He confessed to shooting your brother and killing somebody else. Said he was armed, and he wanted to talk. But—and this is a big one—he will only talk to you."

Max opened his mouth but paused when he heard his name being called from behind the house. He recognized the voice immediately. Steven Black.

"Max, I know you're out there. Tell the police to stay back and nobody else will get hurt." Steven's voice sounded eerily calm and detached, as if he hadn't just shot his brother in cold blood minutes earlier, Max thought. "You need to walk around the side of the house toward the back, so we can talk face-to-face."

"Black, we can talk, but you need to come out unarmed. Turn yourself in." Max tried his best to disguise the rage he felt toward the man who may have murdered his brother. His hands fisted, he resisted the urge to grab a gun from one of the nearby officers, race around the corner of the house and blow the bastard's brains out. The temptation was so strong it scared him.

He reached down and grabbed Theresa's hand, squeezing it tightly.

"Oh, I'm going to turn myself in, Max. You have my word on that. Not yet, though. We really need to talk first. I'm not going to shoot you. Look around the corner. There's something you need to see."

That gnawing feeling was back in the pit of his stomach. His gut told him whatever was around that corner, it wasn't something he wanted to see. But Max had never taken the coward's way out, and he wasn't going to now. He stalked forward, shaking off Wheeler's hand when he attempted to stop him.

"Max, don't," Theresa called to him. He didn't stop. He couldn't. He had to see if what his instincts were screaming was correct.

He lifted his hands to shoulder level so Steven could see he was unarmed, then stepped around the corner of the house and looked toward the back.

A stand-alone converted garage dominated the backyard, hidden from view by the house itself. It wasn't visible from the street. Nothing unusual about that. What was unusual was the scene in the open doorway.

Steven Black wasn't alone. In front of him stood Tommy Saunders. Steven was positioned slightly behind him, effectively using Tommy's body as a shield. His right hand still held the gun he'd used to shoot Remy. That same gun was now pointed straight at Tommy's head.

Chapter Twenty-Nine

Tommy's whole body shook. He couldn't seem to make it stop. He'd never seen a real gun before. Sure, everybody in Louisiana had shotguns for hunting. This was way different though. This one was pressed against his temple, the cool steel emphasizing the reality of the danger he was facing.

Moments earlier, Steven had run into the room, gasping. He and Becca had been listening to some of the country music she liked. A slow Reba song played as Becca crooned along singing slightly off-key. It was kind of sweet. He'd sat with his eyes closed, letting the beat and the rhythm of the words float over him. They were still trying to come up with a workable plan to get away. He'd finally managed to convince Becca they had no choice. Her uncle was stark-raving bonkers, and they had to escape.

Steven had looked between the two of them, then grabbed Tommy by the arm and dragged him to the door. Tommy struggled at first, twisted in his grasp, tried to wrench free, but quickly stopped when Steven placed the barrel of the gun against his head.

"Keep your mouth shut and walk to the door. Just stand there. Not a word, understand?" There was a high-pitched tone to Steven's voice that scared Tommy spitless. Frightened him to his core. Clamping his teeth together, he walked to the open doorway.

Steven stood close behind, shielding himself with Tommy's tall, thin frame.

Outside, police officers were everywhere. By the edge of the house. Behind the fence. He even spotted a couple on the roof of the house. All armed. Sunlight glinted off their guns. Guns pointed directly at him. Tommy swallowed hard, his mouth suddenly dry. *This is it; something's going down now.*

Steven called his godfather's name. *Uncle Max.* His breath caught in his chest when he heard Max answer Steven's yell, trying to talk him into coming out and turning himself in to the police.

Steven had answered something back, but Tommy stopped listening to the words. His mind raced as he held himself tense, alert. This madness would end now. With the police and Uncle Max here, he'd be going home soon. At least he prayed both he and Becca would get out of this endless nightmare. He just had to stay calm and be ready when the time came to make his move.

Steven pressed the pistol harder against his temple, making sure Max could see it. Tommy winced when the cold barrel dug into his skin, hard enough to hurt. His eyes cut to the policeman on the roof, rifle aimed at him. He knew the cops weren't really pointing at *him.* They were trying to get a clear shot at Steven. Steven might be crazy, but Tommy knew he wasn't stupid. He was using Tommy as protection.

"Tommy, you okay?" Max's voice rang out clearly across

the yard, concern evident with each word.

Tommy shifted his stance, but remained silent, awaiting Steven's permission to answer.

"Go ahead. Tell him I've been treating you well."

"I'm fine, Uncle Max. Mr. Black hasn't hurt me. He's been…" Tommy's voice cracked. "Taking good care of me." He had to start over to get the words out.

"We're gonna get you out of there, son. You'll be home before you know it."

Tommy couldn't contain the sob that broke free at Max's words. *Home.* He'd been so unhappy there for the last few months, now it was the only place he wanted to be.

Steven shifted slightly behind him, distributing his weight from foot to foot. Tommy kept his eyes centered on Max.

"I'm sorry about your brother, Max." Steven cleared his throat. "If he'd just minded his own business and left when I'd asked, things wouldn't have come to this. I had everything planned out, to the last detail. I just needed a few more days. Your brother ruined everything. That's why I had to shoot him."

Tommy's back stiffened ramrod straight. *When had that happened?*

"Remy is a police officer, Black. He was doing his job, helping another family find their missing son. The son you killed, you sorry son of a bitch." Anger overrode the calm of his voice. Max took a step forward, but an officer grabbed his arm, keeping him where he was.

"I'm really sorry about that. I never meant to hurt the

boy. He saw Tommy and wanted to run to the police. I had to stop him. You understand, don't you, I had to stop the screaming." Tommy's knees shook slightly but he locked them tight. Hearing that high-pitched tone in Steven's voice, even without being able to see him, he could tell Steven was losing it.

"Sure, Steven, I can understand that. I'm sure it was an accident. I'll be sure to tell his parents how sorry you are when I tell them their son is dead."

Tommy felt Steven flinch, but the barrel of the gun stayed firmly pressed against his head. He was terrified to move at all, fearful that, with Steven so jumpy, the gun might go off accidentally.

"Look, Steven, if you just let Tommy go, I'll make sure everybody knows you treated him well, that you cooperated with the police. You need to let him come out here. Put the gun on the ground and step back. I promise nobody will get hurt." Back was the calm, soothing Max, controlled under pressure, his voice smooth as silk. From his tone, you'd think Steven was his best buddy and he was here to help him out of a bad situation.

"You know I can't do that, Max. The second I move away from Tommy, those policemen on the roof or along the fence are going to blow me away."

"No, they won't, not if you turn yourself in. These men don't want to shoot you. They are trained professionals. They won't shoot unless provoked. You're not going to provoke them now, are you, Steven?"

"Max, tell them I'm thinking about it, okay? I need a few

minutes. Can you get me a few minutes?”

“I’m sure since you’re cooperating, that’s not going to be a problem. Just stay where you are, I’ll be right back. All right?” Tommy watched Max jog around the side of the house and out of view. He didn’t think there was a chance in hell they’d give Steven time, but he’d be damned if he’d give up hope now. This was his last chance. He needed to be prepared, ready to save himself…and Becca.

“Uncle Steven, why are you doing this?” Becca’s tearful voice came from close behind him. Steven knew she didn’t understand, but right now he didn’t have the time to explain. Everything was almost over. Maybe one day she’d understand and forgive him. He doubted it, though. “Not now, Becca. Later, I’ll explain everything later.”

“No, you won’t. You never explain anything. You never have.” Her voice faded away, as she wheeled her chair back farther into the recesses of the room. His heart tightened in his chest, knowing she wanted to be as far away from him as possible.

Max’s voice sounded from around the corner of the house. “Steven, I’m coming back around. Stay calm, everything’s going to be okay.” He walked slowly back into view, his hands again raised to shoulder height, no gun evident.

“Okay, you’ve got a few minutes, five maximum. What are you going to do with the time?”

“We’re going back inside. No shooting or anything, I

promise. I just need a minute to talk to Tommy and Becca, then we're all coming out."

Pulling Tommy with him, Steven backed them into the garage. He swung the door closed, even as Max yelled, "No, don't!"

Steven lowered the gun from Tommy's head and allowed him to walk over to Becca, watching as she reached up to link hands with Tommy. He squeezed hers gently before letting go and walking around to stand behind her chair, his hands resting on her shoulders, a slight measure of comfort. Steven's smile was tinged with regret.

"I know you both don't understand any of this, and maybe you never will. I just want you to remember, honey, I promised to take care of you, and I've done the best I can."

He looked over at Tommy, standing straight and tall behind his niece. "Tommy, you're a fine young man, with a promising future ahead of you. I know you think I'm a monster. You're right, I am. I've done unthinkable things, but they end here, today."

Reaching into his pocket, he pulled out a silver key and tossed it into the air. Tommy reached out to catch it. The key to the lock on his shackles. He stared at it and then at Steven, the knowledge that he held his freedom in his hand sinking in.

He slowly bent down, inserting the key into the lock. It twisted and a click was heard as the lock popped open. He slid the chain off his foot slowly, rising to his full height.

"Why now?" Tommy's question filled the silence that had descended on the room.

"It's time. This was never about you, personally. I'll take my punishment for the choices I've made. I took your choices away from you, and now I'm giving them back." Steven looked from Tommy to Becca and back to Tommy again.

"Choices are funny things. Whether they're made with time and consideration or are spur-of-the-moment decisions, the choices we make, the actions we take, they all have consequences. My choices—it's time to pay for them."

He motioned toward the closed door. "When you leave, take this gun with you, and give it to the police. Tell them I'll come out unarmed in two minutes. That's all I'm asking, two minutes to make my peace, and I'll turn myself in. Will you do that for me?"

He turned the gun handle first toward Tommy, and handed it to him. Tommy wrapped his hand around the grip, the muzzle still pointing at Steven's chest.

"It's your turn to choose. You can shoot me. In fact, I'm hoping you will. Trust me, there's not a jury in the land that would convict you. Or, you can make the decision to walk out that door, and back to your life. Life is all about the choices we make. What's yours going to be?"

Steven knelt in front of Becca's chair, reaching up to run his fingers lightly through her long hair, before wiping the tears from her wet cheeks.

"Don't cry, sweetheart. Things have a way of working out. You're going to be fine. You go on out with Tommy, now. He'll make sure you're taken care of."

He stood and extended his hand to Tommy. Tommy

stared at it, refusing to shake it. Slowly Steven lowered his hand and nodded. Walking over to the door, he pulled it inward, standing behind it and out of range of the SWAT sharpshooters. "Go on now, you two. Remember, Tommy, tell them you have the gun before you go through the door. I don't want them shooting you by mistake. Two minutes and I'm coming out and surrendering. Two minutes, that's all I'm asking."

Tommy grasped the handles on the back of Becca's wheelchair, awkwardly propelling it forward while trying to hold the gun in one hand. She protested briefly, but allowed him to continue, realizing they needed to get out quickly.

At the doorway Tommy paused, the sunlight pinpointing the stocks of so many weapons he couldn't count them all. His gaze went immediately to his Uncle Max.

"Uncle Max, I've got Steven's gun. I'm going to throw it out in the yard. Becca and I are coming out now." Tommy lifted the gun above Becca's head and tossed it out into the yard as far as he could. "Steven's going to come out and give himself up. He wants two minutes to make his peace, and then he's coming out. Don't shoot him, he'll be unarmed."

He stepped forward and maneuvered Becca's wheelchair over the threshold and out onto the grassy surface beyond. When he stepped completely through the door, it swung closed behind him with a soft click. Then, pandemonium reigned.

Chapter Thirty

"He's dead."

Max's words echoed through the hospital room. He shrugged out of his suit jacket and slung it over the back of the lone chair next to the bed before flopping down in it. His hands wrestled with the knot of his necktie.

"Who's dead?" Remy asked from the bed. The whining sound of a motor whirred as he raised himself up to a more comfortable position. His left shoulder was bandaged, his arm positioned in a sling strapped close to his body.

"Steven Black. Lousy son of a bitch isn't going to have to pay for a thing he did."

"Damn. I thought they arrested him. What happened?" Remy's voice was laced with pain as he struggled for a more upright position.

"They did. Once he let the kids go, he walked out and turned himself in. Captain Wheeler was pleased everything went down without anybody getting hurt. Except you, of course." Max grinned at his baby brother, who gave an undignified snort in response.

"Anyway, they arrested him, took him down to the station and booked him. Put him in a holding cell to await arraignment. Half an hour later, a guard found him lying on the floor not breathing."

"Heart attack?"

"Don't know, but I don't think so. The investigators found about a half-dozen pill bottles in the bathroom of the garage he held the kids in. I'm guessing when he asked for those two minutes, after he let Tommy and the girl go, he went into the bathroom and downed all those pills."

"Prescriptions? Any idea where he got them?"

Max could tell Remy's mind was working along the same path his had.

"Yeah, they're checking with his physician, but from the names of the meds, he was on some pretty strong stuff, massive pain medication. Pure speculation on my part, but I figure he didn't have long to live anyway."

"Do you know who the girl is? One of the guys said something about her being in a wheelchair."

"You're not gonna believe this one. Rebecca Burton is actually his niece."

"Lord have mercy, he treated his own family like that, keeping her a prisoner? The man was freaking crazy, wasn't he?" Remy leaned back against the pillows, shaking his head.

Max nodded. "You want to hear something even more amazing? Tommy told his folks as much as he wanted to come home, he wouldn't unless they let Becca come and live with them."

"You're kidding, right?"

"Nope. Apparently they became pretty close during all this, spending so much time together, isolated. When things got really bad there at the end, they didn't have anybody but each other to depend on."

Remy kept shaking his head. "I guess I can understand that. It's kind of like Theresa and me. Friendship through adversity. So what did Tommy's parents say?"

"What could they say? His parents wanted him home so badly I think they'd agree to just about anything at this point. They're keeping Becca in the hospital for a couple of days, just to make sure she's okay. David's contacting Social Services, to find out what needs to be done so she can live with them."

Max ran his fingers through his disheveled hair, making it stand up on end. Casting a look at his brother, he quirked an eyebrow at him. Remy chuckled. "What's so funny?"

"Sorry, bro. You're just looking a bit like a porcupine at the moment." Max's hand flew back up, smoothing down the offending locks, while Remy continued to grin at him.

"Why so dressed up, by the way? Going someplace special?"

Max shifted in the chair, hesitating, uncertain with what he was about to tell his brother. He knew how much Remy cared about Theresa, and he didn't want to drive a wedge between them. But Max loved her, more than he'd ever thought it possible to love another person. Just thinking about her made his blood sing. Desire flashed through him within seconds.

"I'm taking Theresa out to dinner tonight. Look, Remy, about me and Theresa, there's something you need to know."

"You mean like the fact that you're so head-over-heels in

love with her you can't see straight?" Remy laughed aloud, surprising Max. "I hate to break it to you, big brother, but I think the only person who didn't realize you were in love with Theresa is you. And maybe Theresa."

"It doesn't bother you that I love her?"

Remy looked at his brother, his own love and compassion shining clearly in his eyes.

"Max, I care about Theresa, you know that. I'm not in love with her, though. Never have been. She's my best friend and the closest thing I've ever had to a sister. Nothing makes me happier than the thought of you loving her." After a beat, he continued. "You do know that she loves you too, don't you?"

"I'm praying she does." Reaching into his trouser pocket, Max pulled out a jeweler's box and opened it, handing it to Remy. Remy stared down at the sapphire-and-diamond ring nestled inside, surrounded by the black velvet interior.

"I'm going to ask Theresa to marry me."

"You'll wait on the ceremony until I'm out of the hospital, so I can be the best man, right?" Remy grinned up at his brother, then grimaced as the muscles pulled in his shoulder from too much movement.

"How long before they spring you from this joint anyway?"

"Couple more days. They want to keep me to make sure there's no sign of infection from the surgery where they took out the bullet."

"You are so damn lucky it missed your heart. Doc said another couple of inches and we'd have lost you. It struck the rib, and they had a heck of a time digging that sucker out."

Remy rolled his eyes. "Don't remind me. I've heard it in gruesome detail from the guys at the station."

Remy handed the ring box back to Max, as a nurse came in to check his vitals. The cute curvy blonde smiled as she wrapped the blood pressure cuff around his upper arm. Remy grinned at his brother and winked.

Max replaced the ring in his pocket. With a quick wave to his brother, he left him to the tender mercies of the nursing staff.

Theresa totaled up the receipts Maggie had left for her, after closing up the shop that afternoon. Working on the Saunders case with Max and Remy, she'd been away from her place more than usual, yet the customers still came and spent their hard-earned dollars on the merchandise she carried. Whenever she thought about her shop she always felt a sense of accomplishment, a pride that her place was unique and special. Citizens of New Orleans and tourists alike frequented her place. She made a good living doing something she loved, yet now it wasn't enough.

She knew the answer, had known for some time, but she'd been running from the truth. God in His infinite wisdom had given her a special gift—one born in tragedy, but nonetheless a gift—which she had squandered, ignored and even hidden.

She walked to the safe in the wall behind her glass counter, opened it and placed the daily receipts and cash inside. She swung the door closed, spinning the tumblers to make sure it locked. She froze, feeling the air around her turn eerily cold, goose bumps running up and down her arms. Instinctively she turned around and came face-to-face with Jacob Freeman.

Or, more precisely, his ghost. She raised a trembling hand to her chest in surprise. *Okay, you've talked to him before, and he didn't hurt you. Stay calm and find out what he wants.*

"Hello, Jacob. Can I do something for you?"

Jacob was still more insubstantial than solid, but distinctly present. He looked exactly as he had the last time she'd seen him in her dream.

"I came to say thanks. You saved Tommy and the girl. Because of you, he can't hurt anybody ever again. I'm just sorry he won't pay for what he did to them and to me."

"What do you mean? He's been arrested, and he'll go to prison."

"No he won't, because he's dead. He killed himself." Jacob's apparition shook his head slowly, his expression sad.

"He was in jail, how could he have committed suicide?"

"All I know is he's crossed over. I'll be doing that soon, too. I just wanted one more chance to say thanks."

Theresa stared at him. He was translucent, paler than he'd been when he had first appeared in her vision. She realized they didn't have much time left.

"Jacob, I know this is hard, but can you tell me where Steven put your body, you know, after he...killed you? I'd like to be able to help give your parents and your sister some closure."

Jacob nodded. "He rolled me up in a big rug, one of those fancy kinds with fringe all around it. Stuffed it in the back of the old tool shed on the other side of his garage. He hid me pretty well, behind a big wooden table. He stacked some other stuff on top, ladders, ropes and other things, so I probably wouldn't be noticed right away."

"You're still right there on the property? He didn't move you?" Surprise laced Theresa's voice. Poor Jacob had been there the whole time, yet nobody had found his body.

Again Jacob nodded, his blond hair falling down across his forehead.

"I'll tell the police where to find you, and get you back with your family, Jacob, I promise."

He smiled, lifted his hand in a little wave, and in the blink of an eye he was gone.

Theresa walked slowly over and flopped down into her chair. This had really been one heck of a day. A shooting, a hostage situation and, now, a ghostly visitation. What other surprises could this day hold?

<h1 style="text-align:center">Chapter Thirty-One</h1>

Theresa shook out the folds of the dress she'd picked out for the evening. She bought it months ago, on a dare from Remy, but never found the courage to wear it. A deep, vivid red with a halter neck that dipped low in the front and the back, it exposed more skin than she'd ever been comfortable with. She quickly stripped and changed into sexy red lace undergarments. She slid the cool material of the dress over her head, tugging the fabric down over her hips, and fastened the catch at the back of her neck.

She grabbed the hairbrush from her dresser and walked toward the bathroom to finish getting ready. She caught a glimpse of her reflection as she walked past the standing mirror in the corner of her bedroom. She stopped abruptly, her eyes going wide at the sight.

Her long blond hair floated freely, framing her face and cascading down her back. The slinky fabric clung to her curves, outlining them to perfection, accentuating her figure without making her look cheap. She liked what she saw in the glass. For the first time she saw an attractive woman, an air of confidence about her that hadn't been there before. Smiling at her reflection, she finished her trek into the bathroom to finish up her hair and makeup. Max would be here soon, and she wanted to be ready.

When she heard the knock on her back door, she raced down the stairs. He was here. Anticipation flowed like champagne bubbles tingling through her veins.

She swung open the door, and Max stood on the other side, a dark charcoal-colored suit encompassing his broad shoulders. A crisp blue shirt and patterned blue tie completed his outfit, the muted colors in the shirt and tie accenting the ice blue-gray hue of his eyes. The total effect was amazing. She'd seen Max dressed up before, but this was different. *He dressed up for me.*

"Wow, you look stunning." Max's words were followed by a wolf whistle. "I don't think I've ever seen you look more beautiful than you do tonight."

"Thank you, Max. I must say you're looking rather dapper yourself."

Max ran a hand down the front of his tie. "You ready to go?"

"I'm all yours." This time when she said those words, she meant them. She truly was his. She knew deep in her heart she always had been and always would be.

Picking up her purse and a light wrap, she allowed Max to usher her out the door. They walked for a few blocks and she realized that Max was taking her back to the same restaurant where they'd dined at the beginning of this whole investigation, where they'd fought and she'd threatened to quit. She looked up at him, a question in her eyes.

"I felt it was the right place for us tonight. To maybe eradicate some of those old memories, and make some new, more pleasant ones."

She stopped and he did, too. Reaching up with both hands, she cupped his face, drew it toward hers and stretched upward, pressing a brief kiss to his soft lips. "I think that's a wonderful idea, Max. Let's make some new memories tonight."

Max lowered his head and kissed her in return, his lips caressing hers, not in a brief touch as hers had been, but a ravaging, marauding, feel-it-to-the-depths-of-your-soul type kiss. It was as if he were trying to kiss his way through her, to be a part of her. Theresa responded just as arduously, forgetting they were standing on a busy sidewalk in the French Quarter, people milling around them, whistling and cheering at the sight.

Max finally pulled back, staring down into Theresa's face. She read the desire and need in his eyes, knowing her gaze echoed his. She wanted him all the time, it seemed, every minute of every day. It was a need growing in her, one she no longer intended to deny.

"Let's go get that dinner before I ravish you right here in the middle of town." He smiled down at her, at the love shining in her eyes. Hands clasped, they walked a few more feet and entered the restaurant. At Max's request they were led to the same table they'd had on their previous visit. The garden terrace sparkled with twinkling lights, accented by the candles lit and waiting on the table.

They placed their order, and Max told her about the things he'd found out earlier that day, about Steven Black's death, and his visit to Remy.

When he finished talking, Max stood and reached out his hand for hers. "May I have this dance?"

Theresa stood, placing her hand in Max's. He led her over to the secluded corner of the terrace where there was enough space for two people to dance. The light strains of music could be heard floating through the open French doors of the main restaurant, low, slow and romantic.

With Max holding her in his arms, Theresa felt as if she were home. With all her heart, she prayed that someday Max would feel the same way about her. She rested her head on his shoulder, swaying to the music playing, envisioning a future full of love and happiness, knowing that it was all a dream, but unable to push it away.

The dance finished, Max led her back to the table where they ate and talked. When Theresa excused herself to go to the ladies' room, Max pulled the ring box out of his pocket, once again looking at the sapphire-and-diamond ring inside. The love he felt for her was overwhelming. He wanted to shout to the entire restaurant that she was his and declare his feelings to the world.

Reaching into his pocket, he rubbed his fingers across the other surprise gift he'd had made for her. Almost as much as he wanted her to say yes to his proposal, he wanted her to say yes to this, too.

He stood when she returned to the table, pulling her chair out before returning to take his seat. Now that the moment was here, he was shaking like a schoolboy. Stalling, he motioned the waiter over and ordered dessert. Theresa watched him, a seductive smile flirting around those gorgeous sensuous lips of hers.

"Theresa, there's something I've been meaning to ask you. No, don't say anything, let me get this out." Max reached down and wiped his sweaty palms on the linen napkin across his lap.

"We've been through a lot these last few days, and I know—even though we've known each other for years—we've gotten closer through this whole situation. I've realized how much I care about you, and want you in my life. You're everything to me." He paused, gazing into the eyes of his woman. His world. "I love you."

Rising from his chair, Max dropped to one knee beside Theresa's chair. He smiled at the tears threatening to spill from her eyes.

"You love me?" Theresa whispered the question.

"Honey, I've loved you for a long time. I fought it. I tried to push you away, but it didn't do any good. My feelings for you never changed, never even wavered. I loved you then, and I love you now." Max reached into his pocket and pulled out the box. Opening it, he showed the sparkling ring to Theresa. "Will you marry me? Be my wife, live with me, bear my children and love me for the rest of our lives?"

Laughing and crying at the same time, Theresa leaned forward and pressed her lips to his. "Of course, I'll marry you, Max. I love you so much. Yes, yes, I'll marry you."

A huge grin spread across Max's face. He straightened, lifted Theresa out of her chair and swung her around. The sound of applause from the other patrons of the restaurant echoed around them. Theresa hid her face on his shoulder, embarrassed at their public display of affection.

God, how he loved her!

He finally lowered her back to her chair and resumed his seat, but not before sliding the white-gold band onto her finger, placing a brief kiss there once the ring settled into place.

Max knew he was grinning like an idiot, but he couldn't help it.

"I've got one more thing I wanted to ask you. It's something I've been thinking about for the last few days." He slid a plain white object across the table, until it rested by Theresa's hand. "I want you to consider coming to work with me. With your psychic abilities, I think we'll be a great team."

He sat back and watched her take in the inscription on the business card. Lamoreaux Investigations was scrolled across the top followed by the names Max and Theresa Lamoreaux spelled out on the textured white card.

"Really?"

Something clicked deep inside Theresa. She didn't hesitate in her answer.

"I don't need to think about it, Max. I want to come and work with you. We'll probably butt heads, but I think we can make it work. I know we can."

She smiled at him across the table, grasping his hand and intertwining their fingers. Looking down at their joined hands, hers so delicate and yet strong, his large and rough, she knew it would work out.

After all, it didn't take a psychic to figure out they'd find a way to be together, working and loving, fighting and making up, until the end of time.

She couldn't wait for their future together to start.

Chapter Thirty-Two
Epilogue

The murmur of voices drifted out to the balcony where Connor Scott stood with his glass of club soda. He downed another sip and grimaced. Yuck. He hated the stuff, but the doctors ordered him to abstain from any alcohol while he was on the pain medications. While he still hurt, especially at night, he'd weaned himself down to only one or two pills a day. He hated the way they made him feel, hated the disconnected feeling, the lack of control they made him feel.

"Everything okay?" Remy moved to stand a few feet away, leaning his hip against the wrought iron balustrade surrounding the restaurant's second-story balcony. The Creole-French restaurant buzzed with activity, the private dining room reserved for his cousin, Max, and Theresa's celebration. The entire family gathered to wish the newly engaged couple well.

They'd delayed the party until Remy was discharged from the hospital and on the road to recovery, having taken a bullet during the case that brought Max and Theresa together. The case had been tough on both Max and

Theresa. Looking for a missing kid, not knowing if they're alive or dead, always took a toll. Fortunately, they'd ended up rescuing Max's godson, along with another teenage girl. The case had taken an ugly turn for a while, but things were finally back on the path of normalcy.

"I'm good. I should be asking you that."

Remy started to shrug, a pained expression crossing his face. "Guess we're the walking wounded at this little soiree. You look better than the last time I looked at your ugly mug. Must be the bruises." His grin tempered the words, and Connor took the teasing in stride. They'd been trading quips and barbs all their lives, and Connor could give as good as he got.

"You're just jealous because all the ladies think I'm prettier than you." He reached up and gently probed the bruise on his cheek, wincing at the tenderness. "Too bad Trejo had such good aim."

"Captain Hilliard's still singing your praises. Who knows how long it would've been before we captured Trejo if you hadn't spotted him. You saved that man's life, and helped capture a wanted serial killer. How does it feel to be a hero, cousin?"

"I'm no hero. I did what anybody else would've done in the same circumstances. I couldn't stand by and watch that maniac kill somebody and not try to stop him."

Remy raised his glass of sweet tea in a toast. "And got the living hell beat out of you trying to save that homeless dude's life. When can you go back to work?"

Connor spun around to stare at the French Quarter,

spread out below the balcony. The streets swarmed with revelers, tourists and locals, all partying like there was no tomorrow. The sounds and scents of New Orleans were unlike anywhere else in the world and he loved his city. The people below—nobody had a care in the world, their lives free and easy. He only wished he knew what his next move would be.

"Chief's ordered me on medical leave. Says he won't let me come back until the doc clears me. Which I've been told won't be anytime soon. He thinks I need to take some time off. Go on vacation."

"Might not be a bad idea. I mean, when's the last time you took a vacation?"

Connor closed his eyes, trying to recall when he'd taken time off from the fire station, and realized it had been his honeymoon. Nope, he wasn't going there. Those memories, like his failed marriage, were permanently off limits.

"It's been a while," he admitted but didn't elaborate.

"Well, since you've got the accrued time, why don't you go visit your grandmother down in Florida. Last time *Maman* talked to her, she mentioned she hadn't seen you in too long."

Connor took another sip of his club soda, contemplating Remy's words. It had been a long time since he'd seen his grandmother. She'd moved to Boca Raton, into a retirement village, where she could be around people her age, and live in the sunshine and warmth. He missed her more than he cared to admit.

"Maybe you're right. Got nothing better going on 'round

here. I might as well go spend a little quality time in Florida. Maybe even find me a bikini bunny or two to kiss my boo-boos."

"Jackass." Remy's words were followed by a quick grin as Max and Theresa stepped out to join them on the balcony. "Hey, guys. I think I've talked Connor into heading to Florida while he recuperates. A little rest and relaxation, fun in the sunshine. Pretty women as far as the eye can see. Wait a minute, why does he get to have all the fun? I got shot; I should get a reward too!"

They all laughed at the pouty face Remy made. Connor knew his cousin, though. He wasn't the type to sit still long for anything. The minute he got his captain's okay, he'd be back behind his desk at the NOPD, arresting the bad guys. He envied Remy's dedication, his commitment to his job, because he felt the same about being a firefighter. It was part of who he was, all the way down to the bone. There wasn't anything else he wanted to do. Helping people, saving lives, it fulfilled him and gave him purpose. It had been his touchstone, his safe harbor, when his world fell apart and his marriage to the love of his life collapsed in ruins.

"I think that's a great idea." Max wrapped his arm around Theresa's waist, pulling her against his side. "What do you think, hon?"

Theresa smile held a warmth that lit her entire face. She was a beautiful woman, and his cousin was a lucky man. Connor was secretly thrilled that Max and Theresa had found their way back to each other. Whatever secrets separated them before seemed resolved, and he couldn't remember ever seeing Max happier.

"I think Connor will discover a whole new appreciation for life if he heads to Florida. This trip could be the best thing he ever does. His life needs a spark, some excitement, and he'll find it, if he's willing to take the chance."

At her soft words, Connor felt a stir of something deep inside. Something he hadn't felt in far too long. A surge of adrenaline coursed through him, awakening every nerve ending, and sparking a jolt of anticipation coursing through him. It cemented his answer.

"Congratulations, again, guys. I'm thrilled about your engagement, and about the new business venture. May both bring you joy and happiness." Connor slammed back the rest of his club soda and handed his empty glass to Remy. "Now, if you'll excuse me, I'm going to Florida."

Thank you for reading Desperate Choices, Book #1 in the New Orleans Connection Series. I hope you enjoyed Max and Theresa's story. Want to find out more about *Connor Scott and the excitement and adventure he's about to plunge head-first into*? Keep reading for an excerpt from his book, *Connor's* Gamble. *Available at all major e-book and print vendors.*

Connor's Gamble © Kathy Ivan.

A pool of matted dark red blood spread out in a macabre halo beneath the gray hair of Mrs. Abigail Spencer. For one brief moment, Connor gave thanks he hadn't eaten breakfast yet. It wouldn't do to spew chunks all over the poor old woman.

He whirled around at Alyssa's sharp intake of breath right behind him. Damn it, he'd told her to wait outside. Then again, why was he surprised she hadn't listened? The whole time they'd been married, she'd never listened to anything he'd said then, either.

"Connor? Is she . . .?"

"Dead?" Connor knelt beside the old lady, careful not to touch anything. Reaching forward, he pressed his fingertips against the side of her neck, checking for any indication of life. He felt nothing. No pulse. No rise and fall of her chest. "Looks that way."

"Oh dear," she whispered. "There's so much blood."

"Yeah."

Standing, he took a couple of steps back, reached into his pocket for his cell phone and dialed nine-one-one.

"I need the police at the Wayward Wanderer Inn on I-10. There's been a death . . . That's right . . . No, there are two of us in the room . . . Yes, ma'am, we'll wait right outside the door for the officers to get here. Thank you."

Within minutes the familiar wail of sirens drew closer, accompanied by flashing lights. Killing the siren, one uniformed and one plainclothes officer alighted from the patrol car and walked toward him. Since all the rooms were located on the ground floor, spectators filled the parking lot and milled about in the now crowded hallways.

Connor spotted several folks from the tour group standing a few doors away, anxiety and concern clear in their expressions. Mrs. Spencer was one of their own. He knew Alyssa would deal with the aftermath of this tragedy, offering compassion and sympathy to each Whispering Pines resident. Who'd share a little sympathy with her, he wondered?

"Lyssa, why don't you talk with your group while I explain to the officers what's happened." The only thing that would keep her from dwelling on finding a dead body, especially someone she knew, was to keep her busy. He knew Alyssa well enough that giving her something to focus on, a task to perform, made the most sense. Pale, in obvious shock, she went into immediate helper mode. He wished he could hold her, comfort her through the trauma of what she'd witnessed, but he had to deal with the cops.

The people from Whispering Pines Senior Living Center needed to be handled gently.

Damn. First a bus crash and now one of them is dead. How much more can these old folks take?

The clearing of a throat brought things rushing back to the here and now.

"Officers, I'm Connor Scott. I called in the death."

Without a word, the uniformed police officer, a tall, rail-thin Hispanic man walked through the door into Abigail Spencer's room. The other stayed next to Connor. Pulling out a notebook and pen, he got right down to business. That's good, Connor thought.

"Mr. Scott, I'm Detective Taglier. How did you know the deceased?" The southern drawl followed by an 'I'm your good buddy' grin immediately grated on Connor's nerves. Hell, he didn't even know this guy and already the hairs on the back of his neck stood at attention and he wanted to growl a warning to back the hell off.

"Mrs. Spencer was a passenger on our tour bus. We had an accident yesterday afternoon. Slid on an icy patch on the interstate. Veered off the road."

"Yeah, I heard about it down at the station. Was she injured in the accident?"

"Nothing serious that I'm aware of." Connor stood with arms akimbo, looking at the policeman. Something didn't sit right about him even though he was just doing his job.

"She had a bump on her forehead, I think. It bled a bit but she was checked out at the emergency clinic by a physician and cleared. Everybody was, except for the driver." At the officer's raised brow, Connor continued. "Broken leg, fractured pelvis and a concussion."

"Ouch." Jotting down notes, the detective glanced through the open doorway behind Connor.

"The young lady with you, where does she fit into all this? Was she with you when you found Ms. Spencer?"

Connor bristled at his tone but answered. "Her name's Alyssa Scott. She's the Activities Director for the tour group. Works at the senior living center where they're from." The officer nodded again. He gave an exasperated sigh before continuing. "A few of the other passengers were worried when Abigail, Mrs. Spencer, didn't come to the restaurant for breakfast. They sent Alyssa to check on her. I came with her."

"Was the door locked when you arrived?" The officer's question was directed at Connor, but his eyes kept straying to Alyssa, and it pissed Connor off.

"No. I knocked several times. When there was no answer, I turned the knob and it opened."

"Uh, huh."

The second officer came out of the room, pulling the door closed behind him. After a quick whispered conversation with his partner he strode over to the patrol car, his wide steps quickly eating up the distance.

"So, Mr. Scott, you opened the door and . . ."

Connor turned back to the cop. "I told Alyssa to wait outside and I went in to check on Mrs. Spencer. Immediately upon entering the room I saw feet sticking out from beside the bed. When I got closer, that's how I found her."

"And Ms. Scott stayed outside the whole time?"

He would like to say yes but knew forensic evidence would show she'd been in the room. "No, she came into the room and saw the body as well."

"Did you notice anything else, Mr. Scott?"

"Yeah, I noticed blood on the edge of the night stand by the body."

The officer jotted down a few more notes in his bent, crumpled notebook before continuing.

"Anything else? See anybody hanging around the parking lot?"

"No. I called nine-one-one and waited here for you."

"Okay. Thanks. I'll need to speak with Ms. Scott, take her statement. Same last name. Any relation to you?"

"Ex-wife."

"Huh. Amicable I take it."

Connor quirked a brow, refusing to rise to the subtle baiting question.

Connor knew most of the questions were standard procedure, he'd been around enough cops in his job with the fire department to know it, but he didn't want this guy talking to his wife.

Ex-wife, dammit.

NEWSLETTER SIGN UP

Don't want to miss out on any new books, contests, and free stuff? Sign up to get my newsletter. I promise not to spam you, and only send out notifications/e-mails whenever there's a new release or contest/giveaway. Follow the link and join today!

http://eepurl.com/baqdRX

REVIEWS ARE IMPORTANT!

People are always asking how they can help spread the word about my books. One of the best ways to do that is by word of mouth. Telling your friends about the books and recommending them. If you find a book or series or author that you love – talk about it. The next best thing is to write a review. Writing a review for a book does have to be long or detailed. It can be as simple as saying "I loved the book."

I hope you enjoyed reading Desperate Choices.

If you liked the story, I hope you'll consider leaving a review for the book at the vendor where you purchased it and at Goodreads. Reviews are the best way to spread the word to others looking for good books. It truly helps.

BOOKS BY KATHY IVAN

www.kathyivan.com/books.html

NEW ORLEANS CONNECTION SERIES

Desperate Choices

Connor's Gamble

Relentless Pursuit

Ultimate Betrayal

Keeping Secrets

Sex, Lies and Apple Pies

Deadly Justice

Wicked Obsession

Hidden Agenda

Spies Like Us

Fatal Intentions

New Orleans Connection Series Box Set: Books 1-3

New Orleans Connection Series Box Set: Books 4-7

CAJUN CONNECTION SERIES

Saving Sarah

Saving Savannah

Saving Stephanie

Guarding Gabi

LOVIN' LAS VEGAS SERIES

It Happened In Vegas

Crazy Vegas Love

Marriage, Vegas Style

A Virgin In Vegas

Vegas, Baby!

Yours For The Holidays

Match Made In Vegas

One Night In Vegas

Last Chance In Vegas

Lovin' Las Vegas (box set books 1-3)

<u>OTHER BOOKS BY KATHY IVAN</u>

Second Chances (Destiny's Desire Book #1)

Losing Cassie (Destiny's Desire Book #2)

ABOUT THE AUTHOR

USA TODAY Bestselling author Kathy Ivan spent most of her life with her nose between the pages of a book. It didn't matter if the book was a paranormal romance, romantic suspense, action and adventure thrillers, sweet & spicy, or a sexy novella. Kathy turned her obsession with reading into the next logical step, writing.

Her books transport you to the sultry splendor of the French Quarter in New Orleans in her award-winning romantic suspense, or to Las Vegas in her contemporary romantic comedies. Kathy's new romantic suspense series features, Texas Boudreau Brotherhood, features alpha heroes in small town Texas. Gotta love those cowboys!

Kathy tells stories people can't get enough of; reuniting old loves, betrayal of trust, finding kidnapped children, psychics and sometimes even a ghost or two. But one thing they all have in common – love and a happily ever after).

More about Kathy and her books can be found at

WEBSITE: www.kathyivan.com

**Follow Kathy on Facebook at
www.facebook.com/kathyivanauthor**

Follow Kathy on Twitter at twitter.com/@kathyivan

**Follow Kathy at BookBub
bookbub.com/profile/kathy-ivan**